ASIAN WORKERS STORIES

EDITIED BY Luka Lei Zhang

HARDBALL PRESS

ASIAN WORKERS STORIES

Editor: Luka Lei Zhang

Translated by V. Ramaswamy, Alton Melvar M. Dapanas and Luka Lei Zhang

Copyright © 2024 by Hard Ball Press

All rights reserved.
ISBN: 979-8-9898025-3-1

Library of Congress Cataloging-in-Publication Data: Zhang, Luka Lei

1. Asian workers 2. Working class literature 3. Migrant workers 4. Labor 5. Luka Lei Zhang 6. Hard Ball Press

Cover art by 3in

Book design by 3in

Book formatting by Matthew Tallon

For information about the book and to request copies, email: hardballpress@gmail.com

Luka Lei Zhang

Editor's Note

This book stands as a testament to a collaborative endeavor rooted in the working-class milieu, encompassing the contributions of writers, translators, editors, graphic designers, and the publishing house, Hard Ball Press. It represents a concerted effort to forge a bond among contemporary worker writers within the Asian context, fostering a collective platform that unites their literary pursuits and talents.

During my research on working-class literature in Asia, I have had the privilege of reading a plethora of narratives authored by workers themselves. These stories, spanning a range of time periods, offer profound insight into the lived experiences of the working class. For instance, I have come across captivating accounts nestled within the weathered pages of leftist and communist magazines from the 1950s, symbolizing the historical significance of these publications as platforms for workers to express their thoughts and aspirations. I have also encountered poignant tales penned by migrant workers in more recent years, providing a glimpse into the challenges and triumphs faced by those who have ventured far from their homelands in pursuit of a livelihood. I have been immensely moved by the literary contributions of worker writers who, through their sheer dedication and perseverance, have independently crafted and published their texts over the span of several decades. Their remarkable talent and unwavering commitment have enriched the working-class literary landscape, leaving an indelible mark on the collective narrative of the region.

Sadly, many of these stories go unnoticed or are excluded from today's literary scene. Recognizing this, I embarked on a translation and collection project to gather texts written by different Asian workers for a "new" publication. This book represents my first attempt to address this gap. I am worried about the prevailing trend of viewing migrant worker or working-class writers solely through the lens of "cultural" identity. My intention is to emphasize that the core focus of the worker writers is to illuminate their economic role and the exploitation they endure within the capitalist world. Additionally, it is my sincere hope that this publication will foster connections and solidarity among working-class writers in Asia. For the worker writers, you are not writing alone.

Within this anthology, authors show remarkable diversity across various dimensions. Each story represents a tapestry of experiences deeply rooted in distinct communities and is intricately connected to broader social and political contexts. Readers are not only invited to immerse themselves in the captivating narratives of each short story, but are also warmly encouraged to delve deeper into the historical settings, and to discover the various writing communities related to their literary efforts.

The anthology features writers with varying levels of experience. Some have been honing their craft for many years, while others are relatively new to the literary scene. For example, Lü Caiyi and Shengzi can be considered older working-class writers who explore their respective experiences on a rubber plantation and inside Chinese factories. Both can also be seen as "underground" due to their distance from mainstream exposure and literary domains. On the other hand, Wan Huashan and Janelyn Dupingay are younger writers who actively engage with literary and cultural communities in China and Singapore. Huashan has recently emerged as a representative of the Pi Village New Worker Writer Group in China, while Janelyn continues to organize cultural events and activities for migrant workers in Singapore, along with her poetry collection publication. Although they may not fit the mold of worker writers who focus on capitalist exploitation and worker movements in a socialist realist manner, they demonstrate new and divergent paths a worker writer can pursue. A few names in the anthology may already be familiar to readers in Asia, such as Zakir Hossain Khokan, Md Sharif Uddin, and Rolinda Onates Española. Their readers will encounter stories and poems that convey radical challenges both in the literary and political spheres.

The role of translators in bringing this book to fruition cannot be overstated. We are especially fortunate to have experienced translators including, V. Ramaswamy and Alton Melvar M Dapanas, whose expertise has allowed us to read brilliant writers such as Hamiruddin Middya and Stefani J Alvarez. I extend my heartfelt gratitude to all the translators for their generosity and dedication.

I envision this book as the beginning of a larger worker literature project in Asia and beyond. It is my hope that more texts can be translated, collected, and published in the future. And finally, a big thank you to the writers in this collection for everything.

PART 1
FICTION

PART 2
NON-FICTION

PART 1
FICTION

Zakir Hossain Khokan

Rain

Rames took a bottle of water from the side pocket of his bag, drank some water, put the lid back on the bottle, took out his mobile phone from his pants pocket, and looked around to see his colleagues sitting here and there on the side of the road outside the ongoing construction site. They were all migrant workers at this construction site.

Rames quickly pushed past everyone and sat down on the sidewalk to make a phone call to Priya. The phone rang, but no one answered. Priya was Rames's wife, nine months pregnant. Rames grew restless when Priya didn't answer the call despite him trying twice. He wondered about her well-being; why she wasn't picking up; and why his calls were going unanswered. Was she doing okay?

His restlessness and worry about Priya intensified. The deafening noises from the construction site behind him, the chatter of people around — none of it reached his ears.

Rames looked up at the sky, noticing many clouds, as if rain was imminent. Both Rames and Priya liked rain very much. They had named their unborn child "Rain." Priya had once told Rames, "Rain will grow up to be like you — loved by the family, an immigrant like you, caring for everyone in the family." Rames, on the other end of the phone, responded, "No, my child won't be a migrant worker. He won't be a slave." His jaw clenched as he spoke. Priya, oblivious to his plight, asked, "Are you a slave? What do the migrant workers do over there?" Rames felt a lump in his throat. He fell silent and gave no answer to Priya.

Rames began calling other family members, but no one answered. His anger and fear grew. The worst possible scenarios played out in his head. He wanted to scream when suddenly, Priya's name lit up on the phone. A very familiar tune began to play: "Heal the World" by Michael Jackson, but Rames was quick to pick up before anyone could recognize it.

Answering the call, Rames, in an angry and anxious voice, asked, "Why didn't you answer my call? What happened? Are you okay? How's Rain? How's everyone? Why are you breathing heavily?"

On the other end, Priya laughed a familiar laugh which usually cheered up Rames so much. "Why are you so upset?" She said. "Who asks so many questions at once? Listen, I'm being taken to the Operating Room. Today is the day of Rain's birth, and most of our family are here at the hospital. Please pray for both of us, and keep your phone on. You'll hear our son's first cry when you call. Keep praying for us. Love you, Rain's daddy!"

Rames fears melted away, and he was slightly embarrassed by his overreaction. After a brief moment, a different sort of emotion welled up in him strongly: the expectation and joy of soon becoming a new father. He replied gently, overwhelmed with emotion, "I love you, and Rain, too, dear Rain's mother!"

The brief call ended. And there, from his dusty construction site in Singapore, Rames sat meditatively with his eyes closed praying for Priya and their child 6,900 kilometers away in Tamil Nadu, India.

Later, Rames and many other migrant workers waited for the lorry to arrive. Some sat by the road, some talked on their phones, and many lay on the grass — exhausted. Forty minutes later, when the lorry finally arrived, Rames was again sitting in prayer with his eyes closed, waiting for Priya's next call. His colleagues started calling his name, urging him to board the lorry, "*Rames! Lai lai... lorry come oredy, lai lai...*".

Hearing their calls, Rames ran to them with his bag slung over his shoulder. A colleague pulled him onto the lorry. Ten workers were now on the vehicle carrying all kinds of construction tools. This lorry would go to four additional work sites, where still more workers would be picked up. They would not reach the worker dormitory until 10 p.m. The time between 5 p.m. and 10 p.m. seemed to have no value. The workers passed the time by chatting about mundane things among themselves, paying no heed to the dust and debris they were inhaling on the dirt road.

Time crept slowly forward, as light raindrops began to make pitter-patter sounds on the lorry's roof. Within a few minutes, the drizzle turned into a downpour and the sound of rain crashing down on them filled everyone's ears. The sides of the lorry remained open to the air, leaving the occupants drenched to their skins.

Rames kept looking intently at his phone, waiting to hear his child's voice...waiting for Priya's call.

The chatter continued, with workers calling out to one another at the top of their lungs to triumph over the deafening downpour. As they all got soaked, one worker remarked, "Is this what human life is? We get wet, not knowing if we'll catch a fever tomorrow? I've been doing basic duty like this for the past seven months. No overtime. Just eighteen dollars for basic pay. How much can we earn if we get a fever, and we're ready to die?"

Another worker chimed in, "I heard they're going to ban transporting workers in lorries. When will they stop this?"

A screech, a swerve.

The lorry was now speeding on the highway in the heavy rain. Rames kept looking at his phone, still waiting for Priya's call.

Another sudden screech.

Rames barely had time to crane his neck in the direction of the sound, when he was thrown completely out of the lorry, followed by the other passengers all hitting the road, as the lorry itself became a mangled mess of metal. Rames looked and saw spots of red develop on the bodies of his fellow migrant workers, a revolting shade of red which the rain could not wash from his mind.

Despite the impact, Rames' fingers remained tightly laced around his phone. A sharp pain. Rames reached for the back of his head, but his eyes rolled shut, and he fell unconscious. The phone lay quiet in his now limp fingers.

After a time, it emitted a familiar tune: *"Heal the world/ Make it a better place/For you and for me, and the entire human race..."*

Priya's name lit up the phone in sharp contrast to the dark clouds overhead.

"...There are people dying/If you care enough for the living/ Make a better place for you and for me..."

"Call the ambulance!" survivors cried amidst the din of moans and groans and roaring rain — scrambling to help the gravely injured as best they could.

After a few vibrations, the phone's screen returned to darkness. It lay forlorn, drenched in the rain, with no one to answer the call.

Zakir Hossain Khokan is a migrant worker, writer, editor, freelance journalist, photographer, organizer, film producer, and activist — as well as a speaker at TEDx Singapore, Singapore Writers Festival, National Library Singapore, National University of Singapore, Esplanade-Theatres on the Bay, Singapore, and various other platforms. Zakir is also an award-winning poet and founder of Migrant Writers of Singapore, Migrant Workers Photography Festival, One Bag One Book, The Birds Migrate Theatre, and International Migrant Literature Festival. He is from Dhaka, Bangladesh.

Hamiruddin Middya
Translated by V. Ramaswamy

The Grave

The buzz around the *Moshmarar Chawr* grave started as soon as it was spotted it at dusk.

When people of this community died, they were buried at the village graveyard. A desolate place like the "*chawr*" or "sandbar" was not at all an appropriate place for burial. And because the matter pertained to someone's death, it immediately commanded everyone's attention.

It was a freshly dug grave. But the astonishing thing was that there was no news of anyone having died in the community or any nearby village. Whenever someone died, the news spread by word of mouth. So whose grave was this? Who had dug up the earth and buried a dead person in full daylight in this desolate spot at the border of the village?

Puskar's wife had gone from the *Bagdi* or the fisherfolk's hamlet to the canal on a stretch of the *chawr* to catch fish just before dusk. It was the rainy season. The river was like a tumescent youth in their prime; its vigor splashed and spread to the nearby canals and lakes. *Moshmarar Chawr* was not exactly a recently-formed sandbar. It was said that very long ago, the river had been in spate. By the time it returned to calm after inundating all the fields and jetties, it had moved far away, leaving a vast expanse of silt and sand in its wake. Once, a draught buffalo belonging to the *Ghosh* household of *Lagardanga* was grazing thereabouts and it stepped onto the sand to drink water thinking it to be firm ground. The poor buffalo could not get back on its feet again. It sank at once into the soft slime. When the cowherd spotted it after a long search, only its black head was visible. As if it was submerged in a meditational trance with its eyes shut and head turned skywards, or as if someone had severed its head and planted it on the slime. Vultures circled overhead for two or three days. The dogs that fed on carcasses lacked the courage to step on the treacherous slime. They merely sat afar, drooling. That was how the place got its name "*Moshmarar Chawr*" or the "buffalo-slaying sandbar."

There were many branching channels in the vicinity of the sandbar. These flowed from the paddy field into the river. Fish from the river swam upstream. Puskar's wife, Sukhmani, was accompanied by her slobbering son. She was catching *chuno* fish from the canal using a small net. And as the boy was playing in the *chawr* he saw something and came running shouting, "*Ma! Ma!*" He was panting.

Seeing him in that state, Sukhmani asked him testily, "What on earth's happened? Why are you screaming like that?"

The boy pointed to the western end of the *chawr*.

Sukhmani rose from the canal. She put the net down on the bank and walked ahead with the slobbering boy. But he was afraid to go in that direction. He held onto his mother's *anchal*[1] and stuck to her side. After advancing just a little, she suddenly halted and stood still. A freshly dug grave! It must have been dug today. She tapped her forehead and began reciting the name of Lord Rama. Her heart was thumping. After all, no one from their village had died! And this place wasn't a burial place either. It would be dusk soon. The sun had stooped down in the western sky a long while ago. Sukhmani didn't feel brave enough to go back to the canal. Lifting the net to her shoulder, she walked briskly with the boy, crossed the field, and stopped at the three-point crossing in the village. She didn't look back even once.

* * *

All kinds of people gathered at Kartik's tea and snack

---

1. Anchal: The end of the female garment, the sari, placed over the shoulder.

shop after dusk. As they sat on the bamboo bench with their legs dangling and sipped tea. They brought up everything happening in the country and around the world. Arriving there in her drenched state, Sukhmani called out to Giyasuddin Mollah. "*Chacha*[2], can you come here for a moment?"

Giyasuddin Mollah didn't put down the cup in his hand. He said, "Puskar took the money just a little while back. Didn't he tell you anything?"

Sukhmani replied, "I didn't call you to ask for wages, dear *Chacha*. It's something else." And then Sukhamni lowered her voice to a whisper and asked, "Did any of your folk die today, *Chacha*?"

"Not that I know of! Will you tell me clearly what's happened?" Giyasuddin Mollah said.

"Oh my dear, Chacha! My heart's still thumping. I won't tell a lie at dusk when my son's with me. I saw a grave at *Moshmarar Chawr*."

Giyasuddin Mollah was wide-eyed in astonishment.

"What are you saying? A grave? Are you sure?"

"*Chacha*, my little boy was playing in the *chawr*. He spotted the grave and came panting to tell me. And then I went and saw. It's exactly like how graves are made in your graveyard.

Hearing their conversation, a few more people advanced towards them. It didn't take long for word of what Puskar's wife reported to be broadcast in all quarters.

Moshmarar Chawr lay in the middle of the river, with villages on the two banks. All the relatives living in those villages, too, were contacted via telephone. But no one could say who it might be buried in the grave. The whole area was in a flutter. Many people wanted to go that very night to see for themselves. In such an important matter as this, they couldn't rely entirely on what Puskar's wife said, and believe that. It was vital to go to *Moshmarar Chawr* that very night to ascertain the truth of the matter. But who would venture out to the water and slime, through clumps and jungle, in the dark of night? After all, it wasn't easy getting there. There was the fear of snakes at night. But again, if one didn't go, no one

---

2. Chacha: Uncle. A term of respect used in addressing Muslim elders.

would be able to sleep that night!

After the conclusion of the *Isha* evening prayer, Barkatullah the imam from the village mosque made an announcement. "Listen, brothers!" he said. "Everyone doesn't need to go. If one or two people come with me, it's enough." The imam *saheb*[3] had lost count of the number of dead people he had conducted burial rites according to Islamic law. Many people attached great value to his going there. But it wasn't just the imam *saheb*; quite a few curious folk accompanied him, as did some young lads from the local youth association. Some people suggested taking Puskar's wife along. Giyasuddin Mollah turned down the suggestion at once, however. "She doesn't need to come along," he said. "I'll be able to find the spot that she mentioned."

The people of this village that stood along the river returned home after toiling in the fields all day and laid their bodies in bed by the time it was nine o'clock. And they rose almost before light dawned in the eastern sky. But no one was sleepy today. Since the imam *saheb* himself had set out with a squad for *Moshmarar Chawr*, he would not return without fresh news. Everyone was awake, waiting for the news they would bring.

The village was separated from the river by a vast paddy field. The tender saplings of the monsoon paddy glistened under the light from their torches. They advanced along a thick boundary ridge running through the paddy field — a field of silt. When the group left the village behind and reached the riverbank, the evening star emerged from behind clouds and shone brightly in the sky. Clumps of vines and small bushes and stretches of kaash flowers reigned supreme on this bank. A few acacia and date trees stood like sentinels. Traversing through all that, they reached *Moshmarar Chawr*. They flashed their torches in all directions. The old man Ramzan Ali was also in the squad. He was the chief of the village arbitration council. Addressing Giyasuddin Mollah, Ramzan said, 'Giyas *Bhai*[4], go and find the spot. Where did Puskar's wife say it was

---

3. Saheb: A term of respect in this context.
4. Bhai: Brother, a term of respect and affection.

again?'

Giyasuddin advanced rapidly by himself. The western part of the *chawr* was thick with grass after the rains. In a clearing grazing the riverbank lay the grave, dug in clayey soil.

Imam saheb stood beside the grave and scrutinized it for a long time. One by one, the people in the group came up and stood surrounding it. There was a lot of speculation about the dead person lying in the dark grave. After a while, Imam saheb declared, "This is not an adult's grave. I think it's a child."

"You are right sir. If it was an adult, it would have been longer."

"But if it was a child's grave, why would it be even this long?"

"Are you sure it's not something else? Like someone murdered and then buried in this river *chawr*?"

"In that case, the earth would have been flattened after the burial. This is a proper grave."

"Who would have the courage to carry a corpse in broad daylight and bury it here? Had there been no one at all then in the chawr?"

"Hey, mister, why would the body have to be carried here? Let's say he was killed right here. It must be something to do with a woman! Or about dividing money!"

All of a sudden, Ramzan Ali interrupted the buzz. "I think Imam *saheb* is right," he declared. "Perhaps it's a young girl lying in the grave. You know what's happening so often everywhere. Don't you people know what happened just a few days ago? An *Adivasi*[5] girl who was out in the forest gathering sal leaves stumbled upon a baby. Someone had discarded it there. There were ants all over its body. Fortunately, someone found the baby, so she could survive!'

No one failed to understand what Ramzan Ali was suggesting. Picking up the thread, Malu Sheikh said, "There's no reason why it has to be a young girl. It could also be a boy, isn't it? Is there any limit to what boys and girls do nowadays before getting married! What if it was an illegitimate baby?"

The young men in the group had been silent so long

---

5. Adivasi: Belonging to the indigenous communities of India.

because the village elders were speaking. But they, too, had something to say. They were curious. But they didn't have the temerity to express their thoughts. Azfar's middle son had finished college, and was preparing for public service examinations. The bespectacled youth was of a reserved nature compared to the others. When he spoke, no one could have imagined that such a thought would enter his head. He suddenly said, "It isn't a Corona death, is it? Say there was a dead body on the other side of the river. No one touched the body because it was Corona. They didn't allow burial in the village graveyard. So someone came by boat and secretly buried it here."

When Azfar's son said that, everyone recoiled and stepped back a few feet from the grave.

Deep silence descended upon the environs of the grave. It had never occurred to anyone that it could be something like this. It opened up a new horizon altogether. And now began all kinds of responses from different people.

One person said, "But the Corona dead aren't buried. The hospital authorities cremate them. So how would they have got the body?"

Another person agreed with him. "Yes, bhai. That's true, too. The way things are now! Do you know what happened a few days ago?"

"Which incident are you referring to?"

"That one, man, where a Hindu's body was buried, and a Muslim's was cremated. What a bloody disaster, isn't it?"

The young men's talk instilled in everyone the idea that the body was no ordinary one. It had to be a Corona death. But one thing was still unclear to everyone. Which was that when a Corona patient died, the hospital did not release the body so easily. So what was it then? Who was it lying in the grave? A woman who was raped? An illegitimate baby? But whoever it might be, everyone was certain that it was someone who was Muslim by faith. Or else why would they bury the body? So, Imam *saheb* did not tarry any further. He announced, "Whoever it might be in the grave, nothing can be done tonight. Let's wait until morning. We'll get to the bottom of it tomorrow. We need to send word across the river as well. Now we will all pray for the dead person. Please be quiet."

* * *

The next morning, the whole sandbar was thick with people. As if there was a fair going on in *Moshmarar Chawr*. It wasn't just people from this village; people had come rushing there from nearby villages, too, on bicycles and motorcycles. Something like this had never happened in these parts. The elderly senior folk shook their heads in disbelief and said, 'It's all simply astounding, son! What's the world come to? Calamity is imminent! The Day of Judgement is upon us!"

A lot of people were rushing to take a look at the grave. The Hindus took off their shoes, as if visiting a temple, stood afar and took a look before moving away. Muslims tapped their foreheads with their hands in silent salaam[6]. People expressed all kinds of opinions. And each of these were being debated. The young men wanted the grave to be dug up. Everyone was anxious to know who the person asleep beneath the soil was, whether it was male or female, what they looked like, was it someone young or old? But even if someone thought about the grave being dug up, that couldn't be communicated to anyone. Because that was something illegitimate. Calamity might befall the whole village if such an act was committed! The river that seemed so peaceful now could roar like a crazed buffalo and ravage village after village. Everything could be struck down by an earthquake. The entire crop in the field could be destroyed by pests.

A TV news reporter somehow got the news and arrived there. Suddenly, the buzz of the crowd stopped. Everyone moved slowly towards the grave. The cameraman was busy shooting. Imam *saheb* realized that the matter had taken a serious turn. If it had been an incident in a village graveyard, could journalists have arrived? He would not have allowed any non-Muslim to enter without ablutions. But actually, *Moshmarar Chawr* did not come under the jurisdiction of Jamboni village. It was the eccentric river that had created

---

6. Salaam: Salute, obeisance, the Islamic greeting Assalam Aleikum.

the *chawr*. So it belonged to the government. So, Imam *saheb* politely said, "Hello, bhai, take your photographs, but please take your shoes off. After all, it's a dead person's tomb."

But the cameraman was done shooting the grave by then. Hearing imam *saheb*, he said, "Sorry! Sorry! Please don't mind. I completely forgot!"

The camera was now trained on Imam Barkatullah. But it wasn't just him. There were lots of faces behind him. The way the crowd had been swelling since morning, would *Moshmarar Chawr* itself now subside into the river!

The young reporter stood in front of the Imam now, and asked him, "Who do you think dug this grave?"

Imam *saheb* replied, "Listen, if I knew that, would all this commotion have taken place? But it's no one from our Jamboni village, we're certain about that."

"How can you be so sure?"

"You can see for yourself that the grave was dug yesterday. If it was someone from the village, would that have been possible during daytime?"

The camera now turned to the reporter. "That was the Imam *saheb* of Jamboni. Viewers, we will be showing you live whatever happens here today. Stay with us!"

Besides the people from Jamboni, quite a few elderly folk had come from the adjacent villages of Sitalpur and Jhunjkidanga. The leaders of the three villages moved away from the site of the grave and sat under a tree to discuss the matter.

A man from Sitalpur said, "The matter is going out of our control. Now that a news reporter is here, it's going to be a prolonged affair. We need to do something before that."

"What will you do? Dig up the grave and bury the body in your village graveyard? It's better to simply leave it and let things take their own course." That was the view of a man from Jhunjkidanga, who appeared to be some kind of leader.

Imam *saheb* protested at once. "You're talking like an idiot, mister! What do you mean, 'leave it?' Do you know what the consequences will be?"

Someone from Sitalpur supported the Imam. "You're absolutely right. If the matter is taken over by the administration, the body will be dug up from the grave. It will be sent for post mortem. Would it be right to allow all that? After all, whoever it might be lying in the grave, it is a Muslim. As a Muslim, how can I allow another Muslim's body to be desecrated like that?"

Another person added excitedly, "That's right! How can we allow that?"

"Can you please stop that? After all, it could be a murder or something like that. Because of us, the killer might go free. That may lead to the loss of some more lives!"

Imam *saheb* got exasperated now. "Are you in favor of digging up the grave, mister? What exactly are you trying to say?"

The people in the group rose up agitatedly. They were about to strike the leader from Jhunjkidanga. Just then they heard the roar of a vehicle, loud enough to make *Moshmarar Chawr* quake. They turned to look. The leader-type said, "Here comes the police! Try to stop them now!"

* * *

"Stand clear! Stand clear! Don't crowd around here!"

Nandalal Guha, the officer-in-charge of the local police station, advanced towards the grave, clearing the way with the ruler he held in his hand. Two constables followed behind him. The officer walked all around the grave and examined it. He appeared to be quite thoughtful. He took out a packet of cigarettes from his pocket and lit one. After pacing up and down for a while, he phoned someone.

The crowd had exceeded all limits. It wasn't just one reporter any longer, journalists from quite a few TV channels had arrived now. Later in the morning, the vehicle of the Superintendent of Police arrived at *Moshmarar Chawr*.

The S.P. could not arrive at a decision even after seeing and hearing everything. Religious sentiment was involved, so he had a discussion with the District Magistrate over the phone. And then he announced, "We have to arrange to dig up the grave. Or else we won't be able to get to the bottom of it."

The camera was turned towards the grave now. The officer-in-charge of the police station arranged for the digging up of the grave. The crowd around the spot was overflowing now. The two police constables were yelling, "Please don't crowd here! Maintain social distance!"

The crowd moved back following the constable's cry. But only for a few minutes. They crept forward again, little by little. A reporter even reassured them, "None of you need be disappointed. Those of you who can't see should go home and turn on your TV sets. It's being shown live on our channel."

The grave had been dug on wet, slimy soil, so it wasn't difficult to dig it up. The soft clay yielded easily to the blows of the spade. Those who had been able to push their way in through the crowd and make their way near the grave had their eyes peeled. They watched without so much as a blink, lest they miss some spectacular sight! No, they wouldn't let that happen. Everyone wanted to be witness to this historic incident.

The grave had almost been dug up. But there was no trace yet of any bamboo cover. The practice was to dig up the earth, and lay the body wrapped in the shroud at the bottom. This was then covered over with rows of tender bamboo strips, and the gaps were covered with straw before the grave was filled up with earth. Not being able to spot any bamboo under the earth, the man digging up the grave was dumbfounded. The SP *saheb* berated him. "Dig, dig! Dig deeper!"

After he dug deeper, the blade of the spade struck a tree branch with a loud thud. Branches and twigs from the trees near the river had been used instead of bamboo to do the job. Now came the task of removing the branches one by one. And then the real secret would be revealed. Everyone was tense with excitement. Once the gravedigger removed the branches – he froze in astonishment. The officer-in-charge and the S.P. peeped in, and were dumbfounded. They were speechless. Those whose sight didn't reach the bottom of the pit were bursting with curiosity. Breaking the silence, a man in the crowd shouted out, "What's inside? Why aren't you people saying anything? Let us take a look!"

The crowd had reached the limit of its patience. There was pushing and shoving from behind. To control the situation, the officer-in-charge now announced, "There's no human body inside the grave."

"No body? What do you mean? Then what's inside?"

"There's a dead bird lying there."

"A dead bird?"

No one believed that. Everyone wanted to see for themselves.

The officer-in-charge bellowed out, "Slow down now. Don't create a commotion. Come one by one and take a look."

The police officers pushed through the crowd and left.

Moshmarar Chawr was abuzz once again. The crowd surged forward to look at the bird. Why had a bird emerged from the grave? Was a bird something to bury? Who had done the burying? Those who had finished looking were now arguing among themselves as they made their way homewards. Someone said, "This looks like the handiwork of some rogue of a cowherd boy! He must have done this when he brought cattle to graze."

When the arguments and counterarguments had run their course, one man said, "Hey, could it be that crazy birdman?"

Hearing the young man's query, many people remembered the madman. The thought had indeed not occurred to anyone. This was certainly his doing. After all, it was with birds and animals that he occupied himself. "Find him! Find the bastard! If we find him, we'll break his head today!"

The search for the madman commenced at once.

The madman had made his lair here quite a long time ago. He was spotted from time to time. No one knew anything about him. He went around asking people for money, with which he then bought food from the shop, to feed animals and birds. He lay under a tree, or under the sunshade of a shop. On day, he was seen crying because a crow had gotten electrocuted.

Someone asked, "Why would he bury a bird? Is the madman a Muslim then?"

The buzz didn't cease. There was no end to the debate. The crowd began to disperse slowly. In a little while, once the crowd thinned, *Moshmarar Chawr* turned silent. Slowly, little by little, the desolation of before descended upon it.

Suddenly, making his way through the clumps and bushes, a man emerged. His head was a mop of tangled hair, and he wore dirty, stained clothes. He had a skeletal look on account of starvation. Looking in all directions, he advanced towards the grave with great trepidation. And then he began weeping inconsolably. But the sound of his distraught sobs didn't reach the ears of any civilized folk. They only resounded amidst the desolation of *Moshmarar Chawr.*

Hamiruddin Middya was born in 1997 in Ruppal, a remote village in the Sonamukhi region of Bankura district, in West Bengal, India, situated between the Shali and Damodar rivers. Born in a marginal farmer family, he has been in agricultural fields and farming since his childhood. His passion for writing started from his school days. Living among the simple rural folk of rural Bengal, he discerned the stirring in their hearts. He picked up the pen to convey that. He worked as a domestic helper, as a migrant construction mason, and traveled to rural fairs to sell wares. Hamiruddin's first story was published in the magazine, Lagnausha, in 2016. Since then he has written in various commercial and non-commercial publications.

He has two collections of short stories, Azraeler Dak (2019), and Mathrakha (2022), to his credit. He was awarded the Promising Storyteller Prize for the district by Golpolok magazine in 2018. He received the Drishi Sahitya Samman Award in 2021 for his first collection of stories Azraeler Dak, the Ila Chand Memorial Award from Bengal Sahitya Parishad in 2022, and the Sandipan Chattopadhyay Memorial Prize from the magazine Krittibas for the story collection Mathrakha. This book also received the Young Litterateur Award for 2023 from Sahitya Akademi, the Indian literature academy. His stories have been translated into Hindi and English.

V. Ramaswamy (b. 1960) is a translator of literary fiction and nonfiction from Bengali to English. The authors he has translated include Subimal Misra, Manoranjan Byapari, Adhir Biswas, and Shahidul Zahir. He was selected for the inaugural fellowship in creative writing and translation by Literature Across Frontiers at Aberystwyth University in 2016, and the PEN Presents award in 2022. Life and Political Reality: Two Novellas, co-translated by him with Shahroza Nahrin, was awarded the prize for Best Translated Book of the Year, 2022, by the Bangla Translation Foundation, Dhaka.

Wiset Sanmano

Thongphun's prestigious path

NOTE: The story originally written in Thai by Wiset Sanmano, has been translated into English by a translator who wishes to remain anonymous.

1.POR SOR () 2547 (2004)

Famed boxer "Thongphun Unsiri" sat in an air-conditioned bus heading from Bangkok to Maesot, the borderline district between Thailand and Burma.

Since he hadn't been home for many years, he looked through the window seeing things with excitement and amazement.

He saw mountains, some barely had trees, others had evidently been destroyed by explosions. He got frightened remembering how all of these mountains were once green. What used to be paddy fields and gardens were now replaced with ranges of crop plants both big and small. He looked at the scenes depressively.

"Attention please, we are now arriving safely at Maesot, Tak Province," the ticket conductor announced. "Passengers, please check your luggage and belongings, and prepare to get off the bus."

Thongphun got off the bus, and started looking for a minibus so that he could hire its driver to take him to his village, which was located far from the center of Maesot District, four kilometers away.

He was surprised, however, at all the drivers' shaking

their heads no, negating his demands after telling them his destination. He had to further implore them, and offer to pay a prohibitively high fare before one of them nodded his head in agreement. Thongphun had many misgivings.

On the way to his home, Thongphun found that the village's road which was once a simple lateritic/gravel path, had turned into a well-paved and concreted road. All he could do was pray the villagers' livelihoods hadn't been destroyed by development the same way the (denuded) mountains and trees had been destroyed.

"laaaaddddd (the sound of the car's brake)."

The car that ran in front stopped so suddenly that the car carrying Thongphun had to veer away and almost plunged into the sideway. Fortunately, Thongphun, who sat at the rear seat taking in the view, grasped the handrail promptly and escaped serious injury.

"What happened?" a shocked Thongphun shouted at the driver.

"I knew that it would happen this way," the driver shouted back. "I told you that I did not want to come. Nobody wants to use this road. Everybody is afraid of it."

"Can you tell me what happened?" an increasingly moody Thongphun tried again.

"Why don't you lean your face out and see it yourself?" the driver bellowed.

Thongphun stirred in the back seat.

"Oh my god. What is going on there?" he exclaimed.

Hundreds of people holding paper placards and shouting were in the road. Thongphun could't exactly make out what they were saying.

"Brother, who are they and what are they doing here?" Thongphun asked the driver.

"Aoo! Don't you know that they are Burmese laborers?" the driver replied. "I'm already used to seeing them."

"And what for are they protesting?" Thongphun asked.

"Hey," the driver responded without an ounce of patience. "If you want to know, just get off the bus and ask them yourself. I have already wasted too much time. You get off here. Just pay me half the fare. I do not want to go any further."

Thongphun grabbed his luggage. After paying the driver, he quickly walked towards an old lady sitting against a factory wall, selling some food.

"*Yai (grandmom)*," he said, "what is going on here? Why are they protesting?"

"*Aoo...*where have you been son?" the old lay replied while carefully looking at Thongphun. "You are probably not from around here, are you?"

"I come from this village, but I haven't been back for many years, so I do not know what's happening here," he said. "Could you please tell me what this is all about?"

Seeing that Thongphun really wanted to know, the old lady started telling the story.

"Five years ago, when these crops were first planted, the villagers were glad. The plants were big and the villages went to apply for jobs. My offspring joined them, too. The employees working the fields included both Thais and migrant Burmese, son.

"At the beginning, everything was all right. My nephew said things like extra support were also provided. Years later, however, they cut that. The wages also became so low (around 110 Baht per day) that Thai employees could not bear it any longer — and started to resign. The Burmese laborers were the only ones left.

"*Oiii...*these people are bad shape," the old lady shook her head. "Now, they get paid about 50 Bath per day doing the same jobs as the Thais. However, they do not have more endurance than the Thais. But they have no choice, and are afraid of being deported. Such a pity.

"The stubborn and defiant ones went to ask for pay raises — but they were denied. These employees became targeted and their wages were actually cut. Sometimes, their money was cut so low, they became too afraid to ever ask for a pay raise again. Not many people dared to do it again. They were scared of starving to death and being sent back. The owners of the plants won, and cut wages whenever they wanted. Finally, the Burmese laborers could not take it anymore. The exploitation turned too harsh — resulting in strikes and protests.

"Protests like this have occurred many times, but I see nothing improve. If the labor officials come here, the owners of the plants act as if they will back off. The employees then stop protesting and go back to work. Things seem to settle after a protest. However, the trouble soon starts again because the owners are used to exploiting those laborers. It happens again and again."

The old lady let out a lengthily sigh, and then resumed.

"But this time it seems a bigger matter because I have never seen Burmese laborers gather in this much force before. One more thing — the workers have gotten more educated. Do you see that lady standing there who is now speaking?"

Thongphun turned his head to where the old lady was pointing. He saw a slim woman standing with the workers and consoling them.

"Who is that lady, grandmom? Thongphun asked. "She does not look like a worker."

"Her name is Kaeo," the old lady answered. "She often comes here to help workers whenever they have problems with their owners. She helps translate laws...teaches Thai to them...and often comes to sit here and chat with me. She is a volunteer...what kind...I cannot say it correctly."

"Did state officials not come here to solve problems?" Thongphun asked.

"*Oiiii*, son...you do not want to hear this," the old lady said. "I heard people in the market say that the government is now afraid of those plants being relocated to other places — in other countries. I heard that the government is afraid of losing income. They're more afraid of something like that. The government does not care about the well-being of Burmese laborers — unless the workers protest," the old woman spat. "I have never seen the state officials come here."

Deciding not to ask any further questions, Thongphun became frightened when he saw both the police and the army spread their forces over the road. Several vehicles for detaining prisoners stood nearby.

Chaos broke out a moment later when the officials began to disperse the protesters. Thongphun was appalled. He did not want to believe what he was seeing. The police and army were beating the protesters with batons.

"No...do not hurt them," the old lady beseeched them. "I beg you!" The men with the batons ignored her while they continued to callously beat the protesters. The old lady continued shouting and was put into one of the waiting vehicles.

Two hours later, everything calmed down. The foreign laborers were cleared off the road. The only thing left of the melee were the paper placards torn to pieces and strewn out across the area.

Approaching the scene, Thongphun looked at the torn pieces still littering the ground and recognized the names of some big brand advertisers from the posters often put around the boxing ring. Thongphun had, himself, worked as a presenter for one of the companies advertised on the shredded placards.

Suddenly, Thongphun recalled just how much the lucrative pay he received differed from the low wages these workers received — even though they were the real producers. In contrast, Thongphun didn't have to do much more then put on that brand name's shoes and clothing and have his photograph taken to get paid a handsome amount of money.

He also remembered the first time the representative of that company contacted him about the modeling job. That person had boasted so eloquently about the company's morality and how Thongphun could not help but be proud to work with them. Thongphun actually felt delighted — until the reality of what he witnessed today.

Inclining his head to see the remaining traces on the road, the famous boxer spotted the pale evidence of blood and started to cry. Thongphun promised himself that he would not forget this event until the end of his life.

2.BANGKOK.

A phone clicks.
"Sawasdi Krap. This is Thongphun speaking."

"Thongphun, where have you been?" the voice from Thongphun's coach conveyed through the line. "Why did you not contact me? Anyway, it's okay. Let's talk about it later. You have to come to the club today. The manager and I have to consult with you about something."

Thongphun agreed curtly and hung up the phone. Before going to get dressed slowly and without enthusiasm, he asked himself how he should answer his manager and coach if asked about the reason why he never went to the club after returning from Maesot. Indeed, he scarcely went out of his room.

At the club, the manager and the coach told Thongphun there were quite a few television programs that wanted to interview him on air, but the club had not yet made a decision. Both of them were so excited that they failed to notice Thongphun's reaction.

Thongphun listened silently, and then told them to decide, as he had no problem.

In reality, Thongphun wanted to answer his coach differently, and tell him that after what he experienced in Maesot, he had lost all enthusiasm for this job.

The date of appointment eventually came, however, and Thongphun arrived at the broadcasting station early, so he waited by reading a newspaper quietly.

The news about the mob in Maesot appeared in the newspaper, but the report did not match with what Thongphun really witnessed. According to this, there was neither a confrontation, nor any casualties. Unless he had seen it himself, Thongphun thought, he would have believed what the article was saying.

While reading the newspaper, Thongphun heard a familiar voice. He walked towards the voice until he was close to the wall, adjacent to a glass door, which was left ajar.

"It is such an honor that you came to visit us here at the studio."

"No, no…my boss insisted that I come here. The previous work done on your TV programs was terrific, and thus worthy of my company's sponsorship — especially during the Olympic Games. My boss believes it was a really worthwhile investment and extends his compliments. Thanks to you, our company gained more profits this year, and we can raise the price."

"Raise the price? Why?"

"Hahaha! Since becoming a sponsor of your TV programming, our merchandise is more popular than ever, and no one can compete with us. In addition, we have a noted athlete aboard as a presenter who's helped increase merchandise sales so much, we've almost run out of stock. So, although we raise prices, we can still sell it. That means the cost remains the same — but the profits easily increase... hahaha."

"Ohh, I get it now."

"When you interview Thongphun today, remind him to put on our new merchandise. It just arrived yesterday, and has not yet been introduced to the market. That is why I had to carry it here myself. It will be an informal debut...hahaha."

"Thank you very much."

"You're welcome. By the way, I have got to go now. My boss needs me to clear the news about those Burmese workers who protested at Maesot last week. I heard that they were beaten severely. They deserved it. Anyway, keep it quiet because it would impact our profits if the news got out. I must be going now. Say, hi to Thongphun, too."

Thongphun felt numb all over his body. Was he being exploited by doing business with these TV capitalists? Worse, were they now trying to use him to conceal the cruelty inflicted on the Burmese workers?

What about all his hard training and goal of competing for the country's glory? What was left for him to be proud of now?

Thongphun walked out of the broadcasting station. He refused to be used as a tool to cleanse the image of these capitalists any longer.

Sitting in a taxi, Thongphun heard a news flash on the radio about large-scale unrest happening at Maesot, Tak Province. Workers from various plants were protesting the bosses.

Thongphun was in agony. What he had witnessed there was still vivid in his memory and hard to erase.

He decided to tell the taxi driver to turn the car around and return to the broadcasting station. It was time for him to contribute something back to humanity.

Once the interview was live, Thongphun talked about how the clothes he was wearing in Maesot were tainted with the sweat and tears of the workers. He talked about how these workers were not only cheated out of their wages, but also how the bosses treated them inhumanely.

The compère tried to shift topics, but Thongphun said he would be very glad if everyone watching the show would pay heed to the workers, and help stop the bosses from exploiting their workers.

The compère and station manager urged him to stop talking, but Thongphun refused. He was ready to face the consequences of his speech. With tears in his eyes, and before the camera was cut, Thongphun urged viewers to support the fighting workers of Maesot.

He walked away from the broadcasting station, not caring about the commotion

left in his wake. Thongphun made up his mind to go back home to Maesot and help the workers.

He told himself that he would fight hand-in-hand with them, even though he doubted his ability to help anyone.

Wiset Sanmano was born in Lao, PDR. He is a co-founder and member of Uniamity (samanachan สมานฉันท์) Group. He has one sister and two younger brothers.

He worked in Thailand at the Bed and Bath Company as a migrant worker.

Suphawat Laohachaiboon

Stefani J Alvarez
Translated by Alton Melvar M Dapanas

The Autobiography of the Other Lady Gaga & Other Dagli* from Saudi Arabia

---

ON THE DAGLI: A TRANSLATOR'S NOTE

Within the tradition of Philippine literature written in Filipino, an œuvre distinct from Philippine Anglophone literature and literatures of other local Philippine languages, the dagli (see Ang Dagling Tagalog: 1903-1936, Ateneo de Manila University Press, 2007) is a short prose piece which may be flash fiction or flash nonfiction or prose poem, or all, or none of them. It is a genre which proliferated in vernacular magazines, newspapers, and periodicals at the dawn of the 20th century after the Philippine-American War and the Treaty of Paris when the Americans occupied the Philippines and the English language and American literature was imposed by the state (see Empire's Proxy: American Literature and US Imperialism in the Philippines, New York University Press, 2011).

The Encyclopedia of Philippine Art (Cultural Center of the Philippines, 1994/2020) defines the said genre loosely as "vignettes or sketches" which could be traced back to the Tagalog pasingaw, the Binisayâ pinadalagan or binirisbiris [sometimes called dinalídalí or pinadagan] and the Spanish instantanea or rafaga, as "short account[s] ... spontaneous and hurried quality ... [either as] an explicit expression of a man's love for a particular woman, but at other times ... highly polemical, expressing anti-American, anti-clerical themes." My browsing of the 1900-1940s periodicals archive (Manila's El renacimiento; and Cebu's Ang suga, El boletín católico, and Ang camatuoran) confirmed my initial observation that this genre æsthetically ranges from oratorically highfalutin speeches to musings of a heartbreak (or in mine and Alvarez's native tongue, maoy), from societal treatises to narrative arc-less anecdotes of the quotidian. Such are poles apart from the dominant Euro-American short story form advocated by Iowa Workshop-schooled, Rockefeller Foundation-funded Filipinos who brought American New Criticism in our native shores in the 1960s.

Note: Literally meaning "love" in Tagalog-based Filipino, PAG-IBIG, initialism for Pagtutulungan sa Kinabukasan: Ikaw, Bangko, Industria at Gobyerno (in transliteration to English, "Synergy for the Future: You, The Bank, The Industry, and The Government") is the home development mutual fund, a Philippine government-owned and controlled corporation under the Department of Human Settlements and Urban Development of the Philippines, responsible for the financing of affordable shelter.

LOVE

I went to Al-Khobar with my Arab boyfriend. It was the only city with a remittance center that accepted contributions for the PAG-IBIG Fund. I wanted my monthly contributions to be up-to-date so that I could take advantage of a housing loan. The renovation of our house back in the Philippines was my promise to Mama.

Jubail does not have one for the PAG-IBIG Fund. Its distance to Al-Khobar is the same as the distance from Manila to Olongapo—about a hundred kilometers, a two-hour trip at most.

At the checkpoint, we were blocked by policemen. They are usually suspicious of migrant Filipino workers who are accompanied by Arabs, especially those Filipinos who are shaved, "clean," and fair-skinned.

Yasser got out of the car and handed them his National ID card and driver's license. I glanced at the side mirror. It looked like he was negotiating with them. I was told to get out of the car. They asked where we were going, what time we would return, and where we were employed. One of them whispered something to Yasser who then pulled me back to his car. He explained to me what the policemen wanted. He gave me the condom from his wallet. I did not have a choice. He had already made the first move. I yielded to what they'd already agreed on.

I left the car and headed to the police outpost. I knew

exactly what was going to happen next. It was roughly less than three minutes. I got some tissue and wiped the sweat off my face and the saliva off my nape and ears.

I went back to the car and sat silently. Yasser stared at me. I did not look back. He drove at 150.

"I am sorry. I love you...," he whispered while a song played on the stereo.

Habibi ana... Habibi ana...

That was our favorite song. We used to sing it together. I switched off the stereo.

Son of a whore, that PAG-IBIG... my mind was revolting.

But I needed to make my contribution to the PAG-IBIG Fund.

We still had a long way to go. There were five checkpoints ahead of us.

Note: Sexytary, a portmanteau of the words "sexy" and "secretary," is a common, even sexist, Filipino expression to refer to the stereotype of a sexually attractive female office staff. The language has since changed to prefer the politically correct, gender-neutral "executive assistant" or "administrative aid" across all fields.

PANCAKE

I no longer told Salman in detail about me getting fired from the SABIC head office. The issue of losing my job was not new to him. His response was also expected. "Do not mind it. You will always be a *sexytary*," he joked.

It took a month of handover before I officially became Service Management Secretary of the General Services. Throughout the month of Ramadan, I was there being trained by an outgoing colleague. But when the management decided to remove me from the position, I chose not to report the day after. It only took me an hour to hand over the job and its responsibilities to an Indian secretary from another department. I would leave the responsibility to him in the meantime because it would take another week before my replacement arrived. I listed all the documents and those that needed to be followed up. I also gave him my log-in username and password. If he needed to make transactions, he could open my account.

When I spoke to the person from my agency on the phone, he didn't seem surprised at the news of my dismissal either. I was lucky that he was on my side. "No problem, Jack. We can find you a new job," he assured me.

The next day, Salman invited me to Fanateer. We ordered a takeout for breakfast at Kudu, a food chain open almost twenty-four hours.

"What's this? A No Job celebration?" I asked.

"This is a family day," he replied in jest while carrying Salma's cage, as she quietly lay on her box.

We ordered the Kudu breakfast. One styro box comes with chicken strips, a loaf of sliced bread, two sunny-side up eggs, and butter with strawberry jam, and includes a cup of black coffee. That was for me. Meanwhile, Salman had pancakes and tea. We then headed straight to Al-Nakheel beach. Staying in a small cottage, we laid breakfast on the table.

Smelling the food, Salma meowed from inside her cage. Salman sliced a small piece from the pancake and gave it to her. It was as if my pet was a child who had calmed down after munching on food.

I coated Salman's pancakes with honey and butter. That was his favorite. He also ate a few strips of chicken.

We both looked at the sea. We didn't talk about losing my job. That moment, it was a distant nightmare.

A man passed by, a street cleaner. Salman immediately confirmed that he was Bangladeshi. The strands of his hair were a mixture of white and gray. Skinny. Burnt skin in the scorching heat of the sun. Obviously a middle-aged man. Maybe in his late fifties. He was wearing blue overalls. The company name and logo were noticeable at the back. And the blue also seemed to have faded over the years. He carried a sack while patiently picking up empty plastic bottles and cans on the side of the corniche.

Salman approached him and handed him the remaining untouched pancakes, along with fifty riyals he had grabbed from his wallet.

"Saudi Arabia is a country of humanity . . . " I said.

He smiled. "Life is very hard. This old man should not work like this."

"But he needs a job."

"But not good for him."

"Just as I need a job, too."

He smiled again. "But you're beautiful."

And that was followed by our laughter.

Salman had already started the car. I got in, too. He waved at the old man who was now sitting on the bench while eating his pancakes. I just stared at the side mirror.

"May Allah bless him," he whispered.
"And bless you, too . . . " I whispered back at him.
We heard Salma purr again.
"Aha, you need more pancakes!" Salman said.
"No. She needs a job."

Note: 12.85 Philippine peso = 1 Saudi Arabia riyal (June 2009)

QUEUE

I stood in line at Telemoney. It's one of the outlets for money remittance for migrant Filipino workers in Jubail, Saudi Arabia. I have them in hand—the Telemoney card, Iqama, and the amount I was sending to Mama.

The lines get quite long at the end of the month. But I patiently waited my turn along with other OFWs. The office closes at 8.

I glanced at the digital monitor. It said 12.85 PHP = 1 SAR. I calculated the amount I was about to send.

Five feet away, an Arab man was looking at me. He gave me a wink and signaled that we go outside. I followed him to the parking lot.

I climbed into his car.

"How much?" he asked immediately.

"300 Riyals," I answered.

He took us to his apartment. I made it quick so that I could still fall in line. Telemoney will be closing by quarter to eight.

As soon as he handed me the payment, the doorbell rang.

"I have another friend..."

I made it quick again so that I could still fall in line.

The doorbell rang once more.

I no longer minded the time. It was ten in the evening. Telemoney was already closed. I just counted the riyals.

Note: Saudi Arabia confirms 1st case of A(H1N1)

06/03/2009 | 06:37 PM arabnews.comRIYADH, Saudi Arabia — Saudi Arabia has announced its first case of swine flu, after a Filipino nurse living in the kingdom tested positive for the disease. Health Minister Abdullah bin Abdulaziz says the nurse didn't show any symptoms at the Riyadh airport when she arrived last Friday from a vacation in the Philippines. The minister says she developed symptoms three days later and was tested as part of a routine check at the clinic she works at. A second test confirmed the virus on Wednesday morning. The health ministry did not provide the woman's name or give other details. The minister says the nurse has been quarantined and is getting medical attention.

PIG

I hastily undressed and yanked off the Arab man's thawb as we entered the room.

"Heard the news about the virus?" he asked as I was about to kiss him.

"I don't have HIV; I am clean," I said.

"Not HIV. Swine flu," he replied while I was groping his dick and balls.

I was annoyed. Why would he talk about the swine flu now? Ah, I remembered the A(H1N1) virus had spread here in Saudi Arabia. What was unfortunate was that the virus's first carrier was a Filipino woman—a nurse who, after a vacation in the Philippines, showed symptoms of the virus and was bound for Riyadh.

"Because those pigs are very dirty," he murmured while recalling the news. Not only were pigs unclean, he said, but Islam also forbids eating and touching these animals.

"But I eat pig. You know, pork chop, pork barbecue, pork adobo? Very delicious," I justified, trying to make him laugh.

"No, habibi. It's okay," he reassured me while caressing my breast.

My warm tongue ended our discussion. I wanted to convince him that the pig did not do anything wrong. That's why that night, I let him treat me like his pig.

Note: The Al Nakheel Beach is a favorite holiday destination for migrant Filipino workers. KABAYAN, a term of endearment for Filipinos especially when they meet in foreign countries; literally means "fellow country folk" or "someone from the same country." PO (a variation of opo) is a Filipino expression that indicates respect or politeness especially when talking to someone older, regardless if the other person is a stranger. A shark may mean loan sharks, while a crocodile is a Filipino metaphor for corrupt government officials.

THE FISHING

It was the last night of Ramadan when Salman and I passed by Al Nakheel beach. We hung out by the corniche. While Salman remained inside, listening to Fun's album Some Nights on the stereo, I decided to step out.

I went near the rocks that were stacked on top of each other as the sea waves gently crashed against them. I looked at the stretch of Al Nakheel's coastline. Some migrant Filipino workers were there. Their respective company buses were parked nearby. A few had set up small tents while the others were busy preparing their banquet along the row of cottages.

Some of them were fishing. I saw a man guiding his fishing rod not far from where I was standing. He was pulling something out of the waters so I was tempted to approach him. Past six in the evening and it was already dark, but I knew he had caught a fish.

"Wow! You're very good, po!" I exclaimed.

He smiled. "It's just patience, kabayan."

I sat down next to him. Entranced, I stared at the waters as his line explored the waves.

"We were just passing by, me and my friend. I'm happy to see people having their picnic here."

"Yes, every Thursday night, especially now that it's Eid," he replied. "Fishing is also a hobby for some of us. We get to have fun; we also get to have food."

He pulled again at the fishing rod that he was holding.

He caught another fish and carefully placed it in the adjacent bucket. He retrieved the bait that was wrapped in a small plastic bag. Clipped it to the line. Twisted the rope. He rotated and released it again into the waters.

Watching the sea in silence, he eyed the movement of the fishing float attached to the line. He patiently waited for the fish to take the bait. He knew they could be so elusive. His hands patiently guided the fishing rod. It was as if he was estimating the movement of the fish underwater and the relentless waves on the surface.

"Maybe, even if I don't have a job here, I can make a living with this. For my five children in the Philippines, this is already enough for a dinner," he said while looking at the bucket.

"How is your family in the Philippines, po? Last week, there was no typhoon, but some parts of the country were flooded," I said.

"By the mercy of God, they are safe."

"How many years have you been here in Saudi?"

"I have been here as a bus driver for ten years. And I have been fishing for ten years," he joked.

Then I heard his companion calling him.

"Let's eat! Let's go!" A man called from behind us.

"Kabayan, let's eat," he invited me.

"Thank you, po, but I just had my dinner."

"Life is hard in our country, not only because of the storms but also because of the lack of jobs. There, you also can't find a sea like this where you just sit and wait while holding the fishing rod and before you know it, you already have food," he told me as he put away his belongings. "It's hard to fish in there. If there are no sharks, there will be crocodiles," he said jokingly, before he bid his farewell.

I stepped onto the rocks again. I realized that for those who think of it only as a hobby, it's indeed very tempting to go fishing here. It's a different story in the Philippines, though. And that's why some of us learned how to catch fish in the desert.

HEAT

I woke up from the searing heat of my bedroom. I checked the air conditioning. It wasn't working. On the desk clock, 11:30 a.m. and 39 degrees Celsius.

Katrina, my pet cat, was moving with unease. She snarled sharply. She also felt the heat. So I put her inside her cage and then into the hallway.

I tried to fix the air conditioner but to no avail. I flicked on the thermostat but nothing happened, not even the compressor was functioning. It let off a feverish steam.

I dialed a friend's number to ask for help. But no one picked up.

I left my unit. I lingered in the hallway. Then I caught sight of the sliding windows left ajar in the other building. An Arab man. Smoking a cigarette.

I went down the building. Minutes later, the Arab man was standing by the entrance of the building opposite.

We leered at each other. The heat there in my unit and outside were the same kind of burning.

I lugged Katrina's cage inside into a cool apartment unit.

"Come inside," said the Arab man as he fondled Katrina.

"Beautiful cat." My cat meowed. Purred and purred. Maybe because she's not used to being in here. Maybe some bestial instinct.

And like Katrina, I meowed and meowed all night.

HASIB

On the way home from the office, I rode a cab that was passing by Al-Rashid Mall along Dharan highway. A tarpaulin at the mall's façade: SALE UP TO 70% OFF. I smiled at the sight. I'd like to fully avail of the sea freight that costs 475 Saudi Arabian riyals, almost five thousand in Philippine pesos. The rate is uniform for every baggage, loaded or light, as long as it is of medium size.

So I didn't head straight to my apartment. Instead, I resolved to make a stop at the said mall, one of the largest here in Al-Khobar, Saudi Arabia. It's also frequented mostly by Saudis so I rarely come here. On those occasional instances, I would only go to Jarir Bookstore where I typically buy books. Retailer outlets of clothing lines like Zara, Mango, and H&M are here as well. So, on a big sale day who wouldn't be tempted to shop? In my mind, I thought of the bags, blouses, and sandals I would purchase for Mama. Doll shoes for my two teenage nieces who are currently in college. And other items that can be bought cheap at a discount.

But when I took off of the cab at Gate 2, I heard catcalls from behind me. "Filipini! Filipini!" I turned to look at them. Three Saudi teenagers. Here comes the dogs again, I thought.

I rushed into the mall. As I expected, they dogged after me. Zara is at the entrance of the gate I came in through earlier. Two of the Saudis pretended to be looking around the boutique while another one stood in front of the store. I tried to lead them astray. But they had canine-sharp sense of smell. I went to Sephora next. There they were, outside the store, waiting. After countless boutiques, they still didn't leave me alone. I decided I've had enough. I would just head home. I rushed into the elevator. But they still dogged after me. Inside, there were six of us. With us, a Saudi couple who came out to the 1st floor. I would have gone after them but the two Saudis pulled my shopping bags. That started the chaos. The elevator door opened to the parking area. Like a tug-of-war, they snatched my shopping bags. One of them pulled me into the back of a GMC truck. I fought back. There, I dropped my bags.

They wanted to take my clothes off. On all fours, I begged and begged for them to stop but they didn't. Then, out of nowhere, two security personnel approached us.

I was escorted to the management office. A mutawah, or religious police, was also there. He took my iqama [ID]. Then began the interrogation. What happened, why I went crazy and made a scene. One by one, the shopping bags I carried were opened. One by one, the clothes, shoes, cosmetics, and accessories they picked from the bags, all for women.

"Confess and you can go home."

"But they are the one who harassed me," I defended myself. "Wallah, I just came here for shopping."

He handed me a piece of paper. All written in Arabic. I understood nothing in there except the commas and full stops. He coerced me into signing the complaint filed by the three Saudis against me.

I shook my head in disbelief.

"Gays here in Saudi Arabia are for raping and for killing," the mutawah said as he passed on a ballpoint pen my way.

There were tears in my eyes. Outside, I may have heard the howling echoes of the dogs.

Stefani J Alvarez (she/her) is a transgender woman and from 2008 until 2022, a migrant worker based in Jubail and Al-Khobar, Saudi Arabia. At the annual Philippine National Book Awards, her collection Ang Autobiografia ng Ibang Lady Gaga (Visprint, 2015) [The Autobiography of the Other Lady Gaga] won Best Book of Nonfiction Prose in Filipino and her coming-of-age novel Kagay-an, At Isang Pag-Ibig sa Panahon ng All-Out War (Psicom-Literati, 2018) [Cagayan, and a Love in the Time of an All-Out War] was a finalist in the Best Book of Short Fiction in Filipino category. She also edited Saan Man: Mga Kuwento sa Biyahe, Bagahe, at Balikbayan Box (PageJump, 2017) [Elsewhere: Stories from the Trip, Baggage, and Balikbayan Box], an anthology of short prose, and co-authored Si Mimi at Si Miming (Vibal, 2020) [Mimi and Miming], an illustrated children's book. Her projects received grants from the International Studio & Curatorial Program in the USA, the Goethe-Institut in Dubai, the CLIP LGBTQ+ Network in the UK, and recently, the Akademie Schloss Solitude in Germany. Her latest books include Lama Sabactani: Isang Nobela (Psicom, 2020) [Lama Sabactani: A Novel], her second and latest novel, and the sequel to her first book Ang Autobiografia ng Ibang Lady Gaga: Ang Muling Pag-ariba (Ukiyoto, 2021) [The Autobiography of the Other Lady Gaga: The Resurrection]. She was born in Metro Cagayan de Oro in the southern Philippines. Visit her website at http://stefanijalvarez.com.

Alton Melvar M Dapanas (they/them), a native of southern Philippines, is the author of Towards a Theory on City Boys: Prose Poems (UK: Newcomer Press, 2021), editor-at-large at Asymptote, assistant nonfiction editor at Panorama: The Journal of Travel, Place, and Nature and Atlas & Alice Literary Magazine, and editorial reader at Creative Nonfiction. Their latest works of translation have appeared in Modern Poetry in Translation (England), Asymptote (Taiwan), Reliquaie: Journal of Nature, Landscape, and Mythology (Scotland), BBC Radio 4 (Wales), Rusted Radishes (Lebanon), Tolka Journal (Ireland), anthologised in the Oxford Anthology of Translation, and forthcoming elsewhere. As a poet and essayist, they've been published in Sweden, China, Australia, Germany, Nigeria, Austria, Singapore, South Africa, Japan, the Netherlands, and Canada where Vancouver-based Bell Press Books nominated their lyric essay to the Pushcart Prize. They currently translate classical Filipino writers Adelina Gurrea Monasterio from the Spanish and Fernando A. Buyser from the Binisayâ. Find more at https://linktr.ee/samdapanas.

Tari Sasha
Translated by Luka Lei Zhang

Like a Wounded Sengkon*

NOTE: Sengkon: The name of the person is taken from the work of Indonesian poet Peri Sandi Huizche, "Mata Luka Sengkon Karta," which is based on a real historical event in which a farmer named Sengkon was shot dead by the police in 1965 after being accused of being a communist.

NOTE: The short story is first translated from Bahasa to Chinese by Yi Cai-Hsiao.

I am a farmer from Bojongsari[1]. My father is a farmer, my grandfather is a farmer, and even my grandmother is a farmer. It is not a dream to be a farmer, but a destiny line etched in our pulses. Aside from plowing the soil and planting rice, the children here do not possess any other skills. Even if you have the opportunity to receive a higher education, fate will pull you to become a farmer, just like me, my father, my grandfather, and generations to come.

My sister had gone to the capital city to work, and she said that even being a servant was better than working as a farmer. A year or two later, she returned to Bojongsari with scars and sickness, having already suffered cruelly in the capital, and her humble dream of becoming a servant could not be fulfilled. My sister became a waste collector, but eventually returned to hometown with a rotting body.

Perhaps we were destined to become rice farmers in Bojongsari. Growing rice here is like growing cabbages in the desert. Bojongsari is not a rich land, and there are hardly any

---

1. Bojongsari: Bojongsari is located in West Java, Indonesia.

water resources. Springs and wells are dried up for a long time. I had to pledge my marriage certificate to draw water from a rented pump, and my remaining assets would only cover the pump's rental. The pledge of my dignity was not enough to purchase fertilizer. When harvest season came around, I had to do everything for rice, and sometimes I got extremely frustrated.

During my childhood, my father told me about the famous story of my grandfather, a farmer in Bojongsari who died at the hands of the police without knowing what he had done wrong. My grandfather, a farmer, was taken away by the police in the early morning and found dead by noon.

"What did grandpa do wrong? Why was he killed by the police?" I asked naively.

"The only thing he did wrong was to be born a farmer." My father replied briefly while watching planthoppers attack rice hulls in the distance.

When I was a child, I was obsessed with finding out what happened to my grandfather, Sengkon, a negligible farmer in Bojongsari who was shot by the police. In fact, I continue to tell my children about my grandfather's story very often. As I pass my curiosity on to the next generation, I hope that they will also find out why my grandfather Sengkon died at the hands of the police, and that his story will be passed down through our family for generations to come.

In Bojongsari, it rarely rains and the river is hopeless. Due to last year's bad harvest, my marriage certificate is still mortgaged. How can I rent a pump again? The failure of last year's harvest still haunts me, my wife and children have become very thin due to lack of food. As our only hope for life, rice betrayed us. When the rice crop dried up, I couldn't help but sigh: If rice is our only hope for life, is it also the cause of our deaths?

The worn pajamas of my wife looked baggy as she became thinner. Despite her smile, I knew she was struggling to feed her five children. I wanted to marry her because of her ample hips and figure. According to my mother, women with ample hips are fertile. It was true. My wife gave birth without the assistance of a midwife. The first child was born while she was boiling water in the kitchen; the second while she was carrying water from the well; the third in the toilet when she didn't realize it; the fourth while she was drying clothes in the yard; and the last while we were planting rice in the field.

My children's birth went so well that I was actually quite grateful, otherwise we would have had to pay the midwife several million rupiah. Bojongsari's last shaman died long ago, during the malaria epidemic, before his knowledge could be passed on to the next generation. Allah blessed my wife with easy labor, and perhaps He just forgot to send rain so I could grow rice.

I was told by my wife that the people from the cooperative where I pledged my marriage certificate had come to collect the debt. They informed her that if I didn't pay the debt in a week, they would take valuable items from our house. Except for my wife and children, what do I have in my house that is valuable? No modern appliances, no TV, no radio, no teak table, no sofa, no closet, we sleep on a patched-up mattress. They can take whatever they want.

I later agreed to let them hold my marriage certificate until this week's expiration date, but where would I get the money? I thought about selling my inherited land and moving to the capital, where I could work at any job, construction site, waste collection, delivery, service, or anything. After seeing my sister's tragedy, the thought vanished. Despite her best efforts, she could not resist her fate. Therefore, I must endure the cruel Bojongsari, a destiny that binds me to the present, and to the future.

A week is not a long time. I knew the moment would come. If we couldn't pay our debts, big men with heavy Honda engines would smash our door. Their faces would be fierce, and they would yell loudly. The five children and my wife would stand in a straight line with obedient expressions on their faces. I know what they feel right now: fear. I could only kneel down in silence, just like my grandfather Sengkon when the police were about to take him away.

"Debt collectors rushed into the house looking for valuable items.

"Take them all away!" My wife's pan or the stone grinder.

We barely had anything! As a human, I pledged my most valuable asset — dignity — to the fertilizer vendor. Nothing was left. It was empty as our rice bucket.

"Calda, you must pay your debt now!" The bearded man in the black jacket yelled.

"If I could harvest the rice, I will redeem my marriage certificate."

They yelled even louder, saying they had mistakenly given the loan to the poor man who had nothing. They grabbed me by the collar and cursed me for as long as they could, then left. Threats were left throughout the neighborhood. The neighbors looked at us with different looks, some sympathizing, some mocking us. There is an unwritten rule among our neighbors: They are unhappy when we are happy, and happy when we are sad.

I hugged my wife and five children and assured them everything would be fine. However, I knew that the harvest would fail again, the rice was unable to grow without water.

"If your grandfather died because he was born a farmer, then probably we will die because we were born farmers, too." My father used to say every time he told the story of my grandfather Sengkon. Like Sengkon, I will die soon. But not by police gunfire, but by hunger.

Leaving my weeping wife and children behind, I ran to the fields. I could not die as Sengkon did or as the rice did. For the people I loved, I had to live. From that moment on, my life revolved around pleasing my rice. In order for the dying rice to persevere, I gave them love. My rice had to live so that my family could live as well, and if they died, we would die, too.

> *I am the wounded Sengkon*
> *Try to recall every wound*
> *In the chest*
> *On the back*
> *On the feet*
> *In the coughs*
> *pestered with tuberculosis*

It was as if I had fallen down like my grandfather Sengkon.

My cough was getting worse, my fragile body was shaking...
and I was just waiting for the dominator to shoot at me. Then
I would return to the eternal land of Bojongsari. I had sold my
land. My wife and children would be able to live off the money
after my debts were paid off. Despite the loss of my beloved
fields, I said loudly and proudly that I would always be a
Bojongsari farmer.

Tari Sasha worked in Taiwan as a migrant worker. Writing is a hobby that she sometimes finds difficult to do behind her new activities now in Indonesia. She works for a migrant worker placement company. She passes on all the knowledge and experience she gained during her time in Taiwan to prospective migrant workers who are about to leave for overseas. She hopes that by helping them to go through the official process, they will be able to get a decent job, rights, and protection as stipulated in the law.

Wan Huashan
Translated by Luka Lei Zhang

A Night on Sun Island

(1)

The machine roared in the late night, muffled and sticky. No one dared to tear it off, for if they did, danger would arise. We felt safe, though bored, listening to the sound of the machine.

I recalled gathering rice ears as a child in the scorched crop fields, the rice crop was cut down, tied into bundles, piled up into stacks, waiting to be transported to the wheat-threshing field to be crushed and removed from the ears. The stubble, with its body and head cut off, leaves a knife-edge hole and stares blankly up at the sky. The field mice, snakes, finches, grasshoppers, and bush crickets that have lost the cover from the straw, run away in a hurry under the sun light, secretly looking for another home.

In my worn cotton shoes, I bent down to pick up ears of rice while sneaking at those big grasshoppers, expecting to chase them when my father loaded the wheat into the truck.

"Look at that Big Gray Head, it landed on the Miao Miao family's rice crop! Hey, Miao Miao, what are you doing? I found it first! Just as my eyes followed the grasshoppers' movements and sent threatening signals to Miao Miao, my father swung his pitchfork and hit me twice in the head. I hooked my head in agony, twisted my body, and fell down. The sky appeared to be crushed into stale bread, and I couldn't get air into my lungs.

(2)

Boom! A deep thunder clap erupted overhead.

"Hi, dickhead, you fall asleep?" Huang Chong cursed in a bored voice as he smashed open the two brick windows.

I jerked awake. The electric motors were piling up outside the window. I panicked, and moved fast, attaching the motors to the fan, connecting to the noise tester, and recording each indicator. The qualified products are arranged to move from the other side of the window. The next step would be the packaging. If it isn't working properly and needs to be fixed, we must identify the source of the noise.

A worker begins the machine press to roll the lid; another installs the spring; another attaches the magnet; another assembles the shell; and another punches the screws — there is an entire set of actions. Once completed, we leave it aside and repeat a series of operations overnight, with the same leads expected the next day.

Everyone is tired, everyone is annoyed, and everyone is not to be messed with. I'm afraid of them. I'm afraid of missing a step while checking the qualified products, which will require reworking. They will roll their eyes at me. No one wants to do rework; it means more work without an increase in quota.

I was originally in the assembly line. After the original noise test guy Xiao Jia left, I took over his position. I heard that the team leader was drawn to me because I was down-to-earth. Xiao Jia was nicknamed "Nerd" because he was down-to-earth.

Nerd was in his thirties and went home to find a girlfriend. Before he left, he taught me the noise test but did not explain how to deal with the rolling eyes.

It bothers me that the motor fan in this cage, made of tin on the outside and sound-absorbing foam on the inside, makes the sound of 10,000 flies.

(3)

"Finally off duty!" they shouted with joy. They had tired looks on their faces, but it was as if they had become gold medal-winning athletes.

I usually get off work, get my factory dinner, and go to bed...snoring contentedly.

They are different. They go to Sun Street for the hustle and bustle, drink beer, and eat fried snails. On the assembly line, they are dialed in with a drumming nerve. They say they are headed to Sun Street for human voices.

Three hills surround an area of open land. The factory buildings are stacked like toy blocks. In the middle of the factory buildings is a large open space with two rows of white iron houses that form a commercial street called "Sun Street." I'm not sure who started it, but this industrial area has come to be known as "Sun Island."

They call Sun Island the "factory of the world," but we live at the foot of a hill. Here, crowds of busy people live, move about, and sleep in toy blocks of varying sizes, along with the tireless ants who search for crumbs that have been left on the earth.

We are not ants, after all. We are on Sun Island — and we make the world.

Right now, I'm not sleeping.Instead, I'm feeling squeezed by workers in blue and black overalls on the Sun Street — like a branch of dead wood pushed up by a wave.

Sun Street is only about a hundred meters long from north to south. I've pretty much memorized the location and type of business for each shop and snack stall along the strip.

There's also a Pink Street nearby with things I've never explored. Seriously,

I don't know what to buy here. I just walk, and I can't get to the end.

(4)

I suddenly raise my head and spot Liu Ruyu. She is a popular topic in the male workers' dormitories. She strolls by and gently swings her hips, reminding me of wild roses in the woods on a peaceful afternoon.

My head feels like a honeycomb hosting a swarm of bees vying to be the first to return home before the rain. It's nearly like a spring river up there. Liu Ruyu stops, as if she has eyes in the back of her head.She turns and smiles at me. She is actually a quiet girl, usually less talkative, and less likely to walk down the street alone. I ask her what she's getting. She hesitates, and smiles again.

"Do you know of a small bookshop here?"

"I've been there."

"Well, yeah. Good kid who loves books."

She winks, mischievously. I just freeze for a second.

"I'm going to read, bye," she says.

"Okay."

I turn my back with the word "okay." She walks to the corner of the street and vanishes like a red dot. Many of Sun Island's female workers are pretty; when they take off their factory dungarees, it's as if the fruit wine has been uncorked. But Liu Ruyu is exceptional. She's beautiful even without makeup, and always smells of fragrant perfume.

(5)

My eyelids were heavy as I walked down the street towards the banyan tree. I lay down on a bench. Moonlight mingled with starlight in one spot, tangling and shining down through gaps in the leaves and painting the horizontal strips of the chair with circular silhouettes spaced out from each other. There was not a single intact leaf in the shadows.

The wind increased, blowing shadows of trees and leaves moved before my eyes. When I was younger, I remember as Grandma waved her old cattail leaf fan, the moon would crawl in between the wooden slats nailed up on our window, casting similar shadows on the north wall. Grandma told me old stories and always had me sleep on my right side. She was left-handed.

Once upon a time, there was a disobedient child who enjoyed playing in the pond and starting fires. He did not eat properly. Then he was captured by the old Ba Zi (the ghost from folklore) and thrown into the frozen lake where the water is even colder than the ice. He asked the local kids to help him catch the fish and eat it raw. The children who were unable to catch the fish turned into worms and could never return to their homes. I felt a chill and instinctively covered my head. I was thinking, "I'm not a bad boy." At night, the children were transformed into grasshoppers and chased through the rice crop.

(6)

"Ay, wake up. It is going to rain soon! Why are you sleeping here?"

It's Liu Ruyu.

"Back from reading?" I rub my eyes and ask, "What book did you read?"

We chat. She talks about her childhood as a left-behind child, while I talk about my loneliness. I don't know what is happening, but we kiss.

It it raining and I kiss her. Her lips smell of wild roses, her hair is wet and brushed against the palm of my hand.

I close my eyes and it seems as if I go back ten years in time. It was a cool summer morning when my father and I went to the big weir in the neighboring village to catch field snails.

My father wore a black, tight-fitting polyester shirt, and I wore a red, white, and black checkered coat. We also wore one-piece black rubber outfits used for soaking hessian bales.

I was short, so the waistband of the trousers cinched my chest, constricted in the armpits. My father pedaled his bicycle and carried me in the rear seat. We also brought an old fertilizer bag containing dry food. There is no woman in the house and we are not good cooks. When we arrived at a spot with water and grass, we went down, and the water was so cold and bone-chilling that I wondered whether we were in the world Grandma had described.

I put my hand in the water, looked through the abundant aquatic plants, picked up a snail and threw it ashore. I noticed that the top of my sleeve was dripping water into my gelcoat, and it seemed as if a mudskipper was rolling beneath my feet. I couldn't stand still. My father straightened, I dipped my fingers back into the water and I imagined my fingers were a group of blind men crossing the road, the fish in the watercress were the cars speeding by and the snails that had innocently opened their lids were another group of blind men.

My heart constricted as I imagined the blind man I had knocked over, and I loosely dropped the snail over the weir.

"You didn't eat this morning?" Father scowled at me. He reached over.

"What are you grabbing at!"

My tugging hurt Liu Ruyi. I panicked and let go of her. There was no filed snail in her hair.

(7)

The marvelous Sun Street is two rows of white tin houses built on an unregulated area between factory buildings. A bookstore doggedly sprangs up in the territory of Li Kee's clay pot congee, Fatty's fried rice noodles, and Ah Lan's two-dollar store. In my view, every book in the bookstore is a golden berry blossoming out of stone gaps, surrounded by crystal light depicting a fairytale heaven.

On Sunday, I had a bath. Liu Ruyu mentioned that she had things to do and needed to find her hometown friend who was in another industrial area. I had to go to the bookstore alone. It was a lovely day. I searched through dusty bookshelves to pick a favorite, I searched through quiet wild woods to find a golden berry. Walking to the end of the bookshelf, there was a girl. She was completely engrossed in a book.

You don't see many girls like these in the industrial area — by which I mean girls who love reading. I'm wondering about the books she likes to read. The small bookstore is stocked with pirated fantasy, romance, old magazines, and the daily newspaper featuring lottery results. There are two fridges at the door selling beverages.

I carefully approached her, and as I drew closer, I smelled a strong whiff of déjà vu, but I couldn't see her face as she drifted away.

The veins in my fingers expanded slightly when I picked up the book, displaying some exquisite bodies and lines punctuated with ellipses and exclamation marks.

55

(8)

Sun Island is only a hill away from the modern high-rise city district. We could pass over it and catch a peek, but I'm afraid every inch of it is veiled.

I'm standing on the hard veil right now, longing for my hometown and wanting to buy some gifts for my Grandmother. Despite losing her teeth, Grandma enjoys nougat. I'd like to go to the huge shopping complex to get some. Grandma will be happy, won't she? The fast cars accelerate across the polished road like rockets racing into the sky. I lowered my head as the sun baked my neck. I'm drowsy and sleepy.

The hard sound of the brakes was followed by a piercing curse, "You want to die, ah...don't you have eyes!" It turned out that a delivery guy had unintentionally ran through the red light, which enraged the owner of the car. His forehead was greasy and veiny. On the passenger side, a young woman in a white dress cradled a small girl in a bow tie. She covered the girls' eyes with her tender white fingers until the man was done cursing.

The delivery guy walked away despondently. He had a job that I used to aspire to, wearing clean clothes and freely moving around the streets. "Ding," the hostess arrives to open the door wearing a floral apron.

(9)

I don't know what day it was. Maybe it was a day I skipped my shift, maybe it was a Sunday, and I couldn't figure out if it was early morning or late evening. It seemed like time and space were blurred. Liu Ruyu led me to the hill, and as I looked into her eyes, I saw an abyss. Even the finest swimmers can drown if they fall in.

"Why are you taking me here? What time is it? Where is this?"

"Do you like me?"

I giggled and nodded vigorously.

"I want an apple."

"I'll get you some."

"I want a freshly picked one."

"I promise to buy the freshest ones."

"No, I want it from the tree. It is fresh off the tree! You go get them for me."

"Okay, when I go back to my hometown, I'll pick them for you, as many as you want."

"Who's going back home with you, don't overthink ... I want it now."

"This is the tropics, besides, it is April, where are the apples?"

She became upset and looked at me with her black eyes, "You don't believe me?"

"I believe you, but now, here ..."

"Over this hill, there are apples. Follow me."

I stumbled, fearful of falling into the abyss, and said, "I believe you."

Hand in hand, we climbed over dandelion-covered hills and crossed rivers loaded with pebbles. We arrive at an unattended April garden, with brightly colored apples lining the branches. With a gentle shake, the apples struck me on the head. I picked up the largest one and handed it to her. She bit it with her shell-like teeth, and the juice spurted out, leaving a sweet and acidic aroma that floated on dandelions across the peaceful field.

We ate and ate, and our bellies grew big.

(10)

"Alas, do you all know? Liu Ruyu wants a man, and she is naught at night.

"Oh dear, hard to tell, she looks like a college student, very honest and naive."

"What do you know? That's just prudishness. She's still doing that."

"What?"

"She reads good novels. You know. Heehee ...."

"I tell you ..."

The assembly line belt will begin to rotate in two minutes, and for the next four hours, even the most skilled tongue will be useless. Nobody gets to be idle. Nevertheless, you cannot gossip about Little Liu.

"You guys talk about people behind their backs, it's not good."

"Yo, look who it is?"

"I say whatever I like, none of your business."

"Stop meddling here! It's about Jia Kechong, he didn't say anything. Why are you showing off!"

"Yes, she thinks of Jia Kechong. Okay, it has nothing to do with you."

"Well, you guys just don't bother with him, I've long seen that he has mental problems, so what's the point of bothering with him?"

They talked a lot, and I couldn't compete. My head was jumbled up like a bunch of tangled ropes with no ends. What is wrong with me? What is wrong with me today? What is wrong?

They laughed furiously as their mouths became twisted.

A girl jumped in front of me and screamed, "Why do you like that demon? She's only a witch. You men have to be careful. Be careful!" She ended up rolling her eyes, twisting her neck, and spitting a long strip of water weed out of her mouth. It was so green and dark, covered in squirming small field snails. I screamed and rushed out to find the door.

(11)

Traffic jam, traffic jam...I was going to be late. I held my stomach. I was still two or three seconds behind. The train blew a long whistle and slowly started, heading north. I couldn't care less. In desperation, a force emerged. The windows and doors were closed so I desperately tore up the green train, which ripped a hole in my hand like a torn shirt. I dove in headfirst.

The train was moving faster and faster, and I was breathing hard. Soon, it descended into a tunnel, drowning everything in darkness. The light turned on. A girl sat next to me. Her face was pale, her eyes were black, and she smelled pleasant. She looked like someone familiar. Who is it? I couldn't recall. She looked at me before turning her head towards the window.

The cabin was bustling, with people eating sunflower seeds, drinking beer, playing cards, and chatting without tops. The overweight boy wearing shorts across from me drooled and dripped saliva from his shoulder. All of a sudden, the girl remembered something and exclaimed, "Look! The moon is full today." No one paid any attention to her, and those who did looked at her strangely. Let's see, it is really round.

Wait, I remembered who she was! "I wanted to ask, are you..."

Her eyes are filled with expectation. "I'm..." With a clicking sound, suddenly the center of gravity vanished, leaving the words twisted into fractured sound waves. I fell heavily, my back scraping the floor and my head smacking the chair's iron leg.

I'm not sure how long it took, but I awoke in darkness. The train had derailed in a tunnel on its route back to the north. Where's the girl? I called her but forgot her name.

"Ay, ay" — I had to shout.

"I am here. Come quickly! My leg is crushed."

I crawled over to the voice, my fingers were sticky from moist water. Glass crumbs stinking of booze pierced my arm as I pushed off a fat body. I rescued her. In the darkness, she chuckled, "You really recognized me?" I didn't say anything while holding her and crawling to the edge to find the window. We were like ants floating on a leaf, swimming upstream in a turbulent river. I felt for the window, as she found the life-saving hammer. We started smashing and smashing! We were exhausted. We were suffocated.

Suddenly, the window opened, and a bright light crashed in from the sky, and I saw a fat boy with bloodshot eyes poking at me viciously.

"Xiao Qiang, you dickhead, go home and sleep, you're fired."

They all gazed at me in a circle and laughed. One girl laughed so hard she nearly shattered her green plastic basket on the floor.

Wan Huashan was born in 1989, has worked as a migrant worker since 2008, and has worked as a book editor in Beijing in 2016. After his time as an editor, he went on to publish both fiction and nonfiction works. Wan Huashan was involved in founding and serving as the executive editor of the journal New Workers' Literature for two years and participated in writing and planning the nonfiction bestseller The Laborer's Stars (2022) as well as other books. He is now a freelance writer and columnist.

Rolinda Onates Española

The Kind of Home & New Year in the Air

The Kind of Home

How was your day? I throw the blanket on my legs and stretch myself in a comfortable position beside Pipi. Nah, you look tired than me ah? So, what's the news? Fine, I'm not gonna wait for your answer. I had a long day. Friday is always TGIF. I have good news and bad news? Do you want to hear?

The good news is I already sent my boxes to my home in the Philippines. It dried up my bank account as dry as the drought season, but you know how I enjoy buying things that my family likes — the Nutella Saga, the Pringles Saga, the Chocolates Saga and the Stuffed Toys Saga.I know my family will be happy when they receive it by next month. Take note, it's not just one box, but two boxes. Imagine that! It was sent with too much love from me. My home will be filled with love. My love from Singapore, though in material form, I know will be much appreciated by my family. I think how my Princess' big beautiful eyes will sparkle with joy when she opens the box and finds all the things she wants is there inside of it. One way of showing my love and letting them feel my presence is sending boxes. Being far away from them, I resorted to pretending it was me that went home.

And you know I sent all my running shoes. Precisely, this is the bad news. I'm not going to exercise in the morning anymore. I am not allowed. Me and my madam had a discussion. You know what I realized after that conversation? That for almost six years, this place is just a workplace for me.

I thought I had found a home here, but it was all in my head, only my thoughts.

I realized there were limitations, rules and laws to follow. That I have to be entitled lawfully, that privileges must be stated officially, but what laws and who are those officials? I realized that working abroad is like being in prison. I was sentence to jail for the crime I didn't commit. I never knew there was a trial. I realized that I can never find a home here, although I love the people here as my family. I realized being a maid away from home is a total change of life for a person.

I realized I can never be a normal person here because they base your entire identity on the work that's printed on your work permit. I realized the word "freedom" doesn't exist. I realized equality is just based on one description. I realized my file was encoded: Maid. On the array of files in the study room where each person here has their own name written on it, mine is not there. I realized I am a mother with a voice in my home, but here my voice is blu-blu-blu-blurred. I realized the quote on Jeje's pencil case: "Home is where WiFi instantly connects." I buy data monthly.

I realized I am talking too much. Goodnight, Pipi. As I hug Pipi, I suddenly remember something. Omg, I almost forgot. Today, I write a poem for you. Know that you are my family here, and I will bring you home with me. In a home where my family resides, love and respect we abide. Listen to this, my Pipi:

> My ever peaceful listener
> Consistently neutral as you are
> My weakest state you witnessed
> My greatest gift I shared
> I told you each accomplishment
> Complained on you each disappointment
> Let you rest for the whole day
> Demand your service at night, I may?
> Morning always a short talk
> Late at night is a deep talk
> I greeted you each morning
> I told you about each blessings

I patted you every night
I whispered each secrets
Was scared someday you may talk
That time maybe I can't talk.
Goodnight Pipi, my beloved pillow.

New Year in the Air

An echoing voice repeatedly announced, "Passengers on Flight PR509, bound to Singapore, please proceed to Gate 7 for boarding." Fatima, an OFW (Overseas Filipino Worker) who has been working in Singapore as a foreign domestic worker just stared blankly at the papers (passport, plane ticket with boarding pass and work contract) she was holding. She'd been sitting still in that cold metal chair since eleven in the morning. The coldness of the chair enveloped all three layers of her clothes. The cups of coffee she had been drinking didn't seem to help much with her frozen state of mind. As she let the time pass, she watched people come and go. She watched them as they rushed to catch their domestic connecting flights. She watched them queuing at their designated gates. She watched them inspect Duty Free items, seldom buying, mostly just taking a peek at those expensive items on display. She watched them disappear, and she watched until the cold waiting area was nearly empty. Then she watched the cleaner mop the floor. She watched the plane staff pass with poise. Countless pilots passed by.

Then the scene repeated. She didn't notice that she had already been here in this cold waiting area for eight hours. She didn't really pay attention to what was happening around her. Her mind flew back, or rather had frozen at Bacolod Airport. That's where her last hug with her daughter Adrianne happened. She wanted everything to stop. She didn't want to see her cry. Adrianne hugged her tightly as tears were rushing down her innocent face.

"Mom must go," she said. "We have to do this again. I know you understand everything now, my Princess. Be a good girl. I must work abroad, you knew that. I love you, that's why I have to go."

She hugged and kissed her, as she pulled her luggage and walked away from her. She never ever dared to look back, so she purposely rushed towards the check-in counter area. She didn't want to see the scene behind her.

Her heart was aching. Her eyes began to get wet, and she had to put on her sunglasses—not of a fashion, but because her eyes felt like they were popping out. She was crying, soundlessly crying, which made it difficult to breathe. She didn't want anybody to see her crying, or for anybody to know she was crying—not even her family. How cruel am I to let my Princess cry early in the morning? Her heart was crushed by the thought that she was leaving her again. Two more years she would not see that pretty little face with two big bright eyes. This innocent child of hers, her life, and her treasure. Just last night, they were on cloud nine, celebrating New Year's Eve together. In Filipino tradition, New Year's Eve is one of the most important celebration in every Filipino family. How Adrianne was overjoyed seeing the fireworks! How Adrianne's eyes sparkled with joy, as they partook of their food. How Adrianne danced gracefully, showing her that she had the moves. How they embraced lovingly in celebration. How she wished not to leave her daughter. How she wished to be with her every day, to watch her grow, to watch her sleep. Watch her come and go to school, watch her with all her love.

Her love had to be more than just watching, however. She could not watch Adrianne starve of hunger. She could not watch Adrianne when she wanted something and she could not give it to her. She could not watch Adrianne with broken dreams because she didn't dare to do something worthy with their lives. Her heart would be more broken by that thought. So, she would rather go and leave her daughter, though she knew her girl would miss her terribly. If she stayed with her girl they would both feel better, but both of them knew that they would suffer financially. Adrianne knew if her mother stayed she could not send her to a private school, where she could learn better than if she studied at a public school. If her mom didn't work abroad, she could not give her the birthday parties she dreamed of. She could not give her those fancy clothes and shoes, if she did not earn dollars abroad. She could not allow her to go to those fancy restaurants and eat the food she liked, if she didn't send money from working abroad. She could not give her fancy things that made her leap for joy every time she sent a big box from abroad. She could not give her this better life if her mom stayed, and that she knew well.

She realizes that in life there are sacrifices and choices. Every decision is composed of those two things: sacrifice and choice. The more sacrifices you make, the better choices you have. She and her girl had to make a sacrifice and not physically see each other for two years in order to live better. She chose to work abroad to give her a better life; not the best life, but a better life than what she had when she was young like her. These sacrifices and choices were based on love. The main root of all is love. The unconditional love that only a true mother can understand. How she would love to see her successful in her chosen field someday. How she would love to see her as a strong person when she grew up, because she molded her into an emotionally strong person as a child. How she would love to see her as a person with confidence and dignity. That thinking made her smile, a gleaming smile of a mother dreaming of the most positive outlook for her child.

Then she heard it again, "Final call to passengers on Flight PR 509, bound to Singapore. Proceed to Gate 7 for boarding." Enough with her frozen mind. She hurriedly packed her things and walked straight to the gate that would take her to her destination. Rushing, she took a deep breath as she showed the airline staff her boarding pass. The reality of her situation struck her. She was traveling now for work. Another journey, another two years, another set of trials and sacrifices—and hopefully, another step towards achieving her most important goal. She closed her eyes, wishing not to dream, but instead whisper a simple prayer. Guide me ,oh God, be with me from the beginning to the end of this journey called life.

"Welcome aboard Flight PR509," the flight stewardess enthusiastically greeted her. "Happy New Year."

"Happy New Year," she answered as she smiled back at her broadly, knowing she had peace in her mind and love in her heart for where she was heading—and why. She was making a better choice in her life—a worthy choice—as a woman, and as a mother.

Rolinda Onates Española is from Bacolod City, Philippines. She published her poetry collection No Cinderella?: Poems of a Filipina Domestic Worker in Singapore, 2016-18 in 2020. Española is also the co-editor of the anthology Call and Response: A Migrant/ Local Poetry Anthology (Math Paper Press). She spent six years working in Singapore as a foreign domestic worker and is now back home in the Philippines. Española's poems have won prizes at the Migrant Workers Poetry Competition in Singapore.

Md Mukul Hossine

Ship Phobia

Recently, I have taken a job receiving hotline phone calls. How strange these experiences are! There are even night shifts occasionally. Last night, I received a phone call. A young voice. Might be a new immigrant. Frightened and crying, the person on the other end of the line pleaded, "Brother! Please save me! Brother, I won't survive, I will die!" I asked him, "What happened? Tell me openly. I assure you that I will help you."

The caller seemed to have lost his mind. Without paying any attention to my words, he went on saying, "Brother, please save me! I have gotten into great trouble, brother!" I repeated again gently, "Please tell me your problem first. Tell me your name and your work permit number. I give you my word that as a Bangladeshi, I will help you by all means."

"Brother, they will send me back to my country. I am feeling very tense. It's been only a few days since I came here to Singapore from Bangladesh. I have a lot of loans hanging over my head. I have a baby girl of only two years back home. What should I do now, brother?"

"First of all, please calm down and tell me your permit number. I will help you then."

He collapsed, sobbing. "Brother, I haven't eaten anything since morning. I am feeling much pain. Please save me, brother!"

I began wondering if the man was mentally unwell. Again I tried to find out what his problem was. But no, he wouldn't say anything except repeating, Please save me, I can't take it any more, they will send me back, I am so hungry. Doubt filled me. Was this some kind of phobia, I wondered? "Hey, who are you?" I asked. "If you don't tell me the actual problem, how on earth can I help you?"

This time, there was silence. Then a different voice spoke. "Security guard speaking. Sir, I think the boy is mentally sick. He just joined yesterday. Ship duty. Looks like he is scared to work on the ship." Ship phobia! The security guard and I had guessed alike. The guard informed me that, except for the instructions provided by the Ministry of Manpower, they could do nothing for him.

"It is okay," I told the security officer, "give the phone to him and I will explain it to him."

The boy came on the line. "Yes, brother. Please, brother, do something. Otherwise, I will drown here." I replied, "You have to be more specific about what you want now. Be quick, you don't have much time."

"No, no, brother, please! Don't hang up. I am telling you, brother—they brought me here from the dormitory where I used to stay. They are threatening me with the police. They will send me back. I can't stay in this place. I feel so scared here."

"Who are they?" I said. "Who is forcing you?" Again without answering, he burst into tears. I told him, "Don't cry. I'm arranging to have food brought to you. You eat that now and we will talk afterwards. Let me put the phone down for now."

The security guard gave the boy some dry food along with juice on my request. After finishing, he told the boy to talk to me again. "He is a Bangladeshi. He will help you. Talk to him properly. Have faith in him and everything will be solved."

When the phone rang again, no sooner had I picked up the receiver than I heard, "Brother, I have been brought to a ship. A huge ship this is, very heavy! What if it sinks? What will I do then, brother? I'm feeling very scared. Save me, brother! I can't stay here any longer."

I didn't know whether to laugh or to cry. But I had to convince him anyway. "Look, in this ship, you are going to have a beautiful VIP cabin. Even if you spend a lot of money, it's very difficult to go to such places. Since you are there, at least try to get through one night. Tomorrow, we will try to get you out of that place. As it's an order from the Ministry of Manpower, we can't get you out right away."

The boy burst into tears upon hearing my words and started saying, "What if there's a storm and the ship sinks tonight? I will die then anyway, brother! My parents would be hurt. Please have mercy on me and get me out of here. I beg you, I plead you. I'm your Bangladeshi brother. I wouldn't complain even if you kept me under a tree. I can't stand it in here even for a single minute."

"It's all right," I replied, "I will call you back in 10 minutes," and hung up. I went off to discuss the matter in detail with my supervisor. "Here's an idea," he said. "As he is currently in the security guard's office, let's arrange for him to spend one night there for now." I called up the security guard again and told him the plan. The officer agreed to it. "Those who are on night duty can spend the whole night chatting with the boy, keeping him distracted," he said.

The boy was allowed to stay overnight in the security guard's office. The next day, with the permission of the Ministry of Manpower, he was moved off the ship and sent back to stay in his dormitory. I hope that boy is happy now—or at least that he has recovered from his ship phobia.

Md Mukul Hossine was born in the village of Panbary in Patgram, Bangladesh. His first novel Dukher shimanaye Sukh (Happiness Simon at Heart's Edge ছখের সিমানায় সুখ) and his poetry collection Apurna Basana (Unfulfilled Desire অপূর্ন বাসনা) were published in Bangladesh. In 2008, Mukul arrived in Singapore and began working in construction. Inspired by the hardships faced in his working environment and the laments of fellow migrant workers, he started writing poetry again. On 1 May 2016, he published his first English poetry collection Me Migrant, which was transcreated from Bengali by Singaporean poet Cyril Wong.

Indah Yosevina

A Tinge of Ferris Wheel

This story is about a young woman named Ningsih, a typical Indonesian young woman from a remote village in East Java who works abroad as a domestic worker, and is the sole provider for her family.

In 2001, Ningsih decided for the first time to find work abroad as domestic worker—and she thought she'd try her luck in Saudi Arabia.

The oldest daughter in the family, Ningsih has two younger brothers and a younger sister. Their parents passed away in 1998, after an accident. As the oldest, Ningsih has full responsibility for her younger siblings. She was only 17 years-old when an agent first came to her house with an offer to work abroad. There are plenty of these kinds of agents and brokers who sugarcoat their words and offer young village girls like Ningsih sweet promises—as long as they hit their targets and collect their benefits, that's all that matters.

At that moment, Ningsih said yes—even though only a teenager. She was able travel to Saudi Arabia after her ID was faked to make her appear 23 years-old.

Before she can go, however, she has to live in a shelter for three months, waiting for all of her documents to be ready—and to get some basic training on household chores. Later, she will come to realize no amount of training can prepare you for the reality of working in the field.

November 2001

One week in her employer's house in Riyadh, everything seemed to be going smoothly until one fateful morning when a letter detailing a story of torture was thrown from a neighboring home and landed right in front of Ningsih while she swept the front yard.

She was shocked. Ningsih picked up the projectile and read the letter. Before she could finish reading, however, her madam came from behind her and rudely grabbed the letter. Even though she had not finished reading it, Ningsih understood enough about the letter's contents to understand what was going on. Essentially, it was a plea for help getting the phone number for the Indonesian Embassy. The author of the letter was a domestic worker who hadn't been paid in 15 years and was being beaten.

"It's a pity," Ningsih whispered to herself, "but I can't help her."

Unfortunately, Ningsih's employers visited the neighbors and got angry. They said nasty things to her and accused Ningsih of being a busybody. After that, Ningsih was always accused of doing something wrong.

"Why is my work always wrong," she often asked herself. Every small mistake resulted in an assault. She was hit on her arms when the tea she brought was too hot; her hand was twisted when she couldn't finish a chore fast enough; she was even struck across her back with vacuum cleaner when she forget to close the balcony door and a little rain got in.

Other torments included being hit across the face, resulting in a nasty bruise around the right eye. One incident followed another, each more horrifying than the last. Far away from her family, Ningsih suffered alone.

One afternoon when Ningsih was ironing clothes in her room, her madam's younger brother called. No sooner had she moved to see who it was, when the madam's brother suddenly appeared in front of her, forcefully pulling at her hands.

Ningsih immediately rushed back into her room and locked it until her madam came home from work.

She also experienced sexual harassment when she went

to a shop near her house to buy vegetables. A stall keeper flirted with a libidinous face as if asking her out. Not only that, one afternoon when she was cleaning the windows of the front room, a person she did not know opened his pants and exposed his genitals in front of the window she was cleaning. The perceived harassment didn't end there. While delivering coffee to her madam's brother who was hanging out with his friends in the living room one day, Ningsih was shocked to discover they were watching porn. She was forced to watch it. The living room door was about to be locked — luckily, she managed to get out.

For almost a year, Ningsih worked hard while being physically and psychologically abused, resulting in more bruises on her face. She felt she couldn't take it anymore, but she also needed the job and was too afraid to take action. Finally, she decided to go to the Indonesian Embassy (KBRI) to complain about the inappropriate treatment she was experiencing.

That morning, she walked from her master's house to the Indonesian Embassy. But her master picked her up along the way. She didn't know why. Maybe someone saw her going for a walk, then reported it to her master?

In the car, her master saw Ningsih's bruised face and didn't ask much about what had happened to her. Arriving at the Indonesian Embassy, Ningsih eagerly wanted to meet the staff and tell them all about what had happened. But unfortunately, she was only able to meet a driver who happened to be an Indonesian citizen.

She told him what had happened. The driver, who had worked in Saudi Arabia for a long time, then explained Ningsih's problem to her master who accompanied her. Knowing the problems of his domestic workers, Ningsih's master apologized for how his family treated her. Arriving home, the master discussed what was happening to Ningsih's with his wife and the rest of the family. Ningsih no longer experienced violence and sexual harassment after that discussion.

Later, however, Ningsih started receiving salary deductions for mistakes she did not make. After two years of suffering,

Ningsih was allowed to return to Indonesia. Ironically, without any money from the toil she had endured in the land of the Kaaba.

She went to the airport with the madam's brother. At that time, she heard that her master left money with his brother and asked him to take her to the airport. But the hope of returning home with some money was dashed. The reason is that the employer's brother did not give Ningsih the money she earned.

"When she arrived at the airport, her madam's brother said, "I will transfer the money later, instead of losing it."

To this day, Ningsih hasn't received the money.

After two years of suffering in Saudi Arabia, and without attaining any justice, Ningsih has decided to stay in her home country — too traumatized by what happened to do anything else.

But life is hard, she's the eldest daughter, and responsible for her three younger siblings. She wants their future to be better than hers, but the only way to earn more money is to work abroad again, and the nightmares of her last experience in Saudi Arabia keep haunting her.

She thinks she might go to a new country, one day — maybe this time will be better.

Ningsih has now been working in Singapore for the last twelve years. It has its ups and downs, but she endures for the sake of her brothers and sisters. She's happy that she can provide enough for her siblings to send them to school and get a better education than she ever had. Two of her siblings are working, and another one is in university. She feels the hard work and suffering she's endured is nothing compared to the tinge of Ferris Wheel she sees in her sibling's faces.

There are many more domestic workers out there being hurt just like Ningsih. It happens everywhere. Some will endure, some will fight, and some will speak out. But some will remain silent in their tears — all because they need to work, they need money to provide for their families.

Who's to blame for the all the abuse — *physical, mental and emotional* — that's still happening? The system is good;

there're laws to protect people, but still the abuse persists. What we can do to stop domestic worker abuse?

End
Based on a true story

Indah Yosevina is from Indonesia and has been working as a migrant worker in Singapore for almost 5 years. She loves gardening, singing, reading, and writing. Yosevina likes writing about love, nature, and the diversity of life. For her, writing is a way to express her dear thoughts and her wild imagination. Yosevina's favorite quote is: "If you can be anything you want, just to be kind".

Janelyn Dupingay

What Draws Us Closer To Home

Life, as they say, will never be fair. That's proven every time you witness your child swallowing her saliva while staring at a box of candy displayed in a grocery store window, and you can't even afford to buy her a single piece.

This scenario drove Victoria to desperately ask a recruitment agency for help in processing her papers to work abroad. It wasn't an easy decision, especially since her daughter was only four-years-old and needed her mother. But Victoria did not want her child to grow up in poverty.

Money was difficult for her, and she needed it to complete the paperwork. So, she closed her eyes and borrowed money from a relative at five-percent interest.

With all the many challenges she faced while processing her papers, she didn't give up. Finally, the day came when Victoria had to leave her daughter behind. Her eyes welled up with tears thinking about her daughter waking up the next day. She would not see her mama — the mama who combed her hair every morning. Victoria gave her daughter a soft kiss on the forehead, and prayed in silence to keep her safe at all times. She boarded a Jetstar plane to Singapore on April 27, 2015.

When she arrived at the agency, it was terrifying. The agents were so hostile, and got mad easily at even the slightest mistake. She couldn't understand why they had to treat workers like rubbish. Especially, since they were earning money for them, too. She didn't think she could endure it if her employer treated her the same way.

Still, Victoria had a strong fighting spirit. She knew she was on her own, and had to be very strong in this foreign city. But life became a little kinder to her when she was placed into a family that treated her with respect right from the start. They taught her about her household duties with patience and understanding. Her personal things were provided, and she was given a good room to rest.

What really mattered to her during the first few years working abroad, was being able to pay back what she owed when she applied for the job in Singapore.

She wasn't bothered by the strict rule against using the phone during the day. She wasn't worried when she couldn't call her family anytime she wanted. She accepted the fact that she was only free to call to them during her day off. However, she wasn't able to speak with her daughter during the first six months on the job because every time she called after work, her daughter was sleeping. And she had to wait six months before she could get a day off.

Things became different, however, when her daughter learned to use a mobile phone and had access to text messaging. But the small child would always message her mother with too many difficult questions that were hard to explain, and could only be replied to at night. Eventually, Victoria started questioning why she did not have the freedom to look at her phone during the day — especially when everyone knew how important it was for her to connect with her daughter.

She started sneaking her phone into the toilet, but always felt guilty about it. She tried to suppress the growing unhappiness within her, until early one morning before starting work, she discovered she was being bombarded with text messages from her daughter. Her grandma was feeling very dizzy and her child didn't know what to do. She messaged and called her mother hoping to get instructions on what she could do to help. The poor child was crying and afraid when Victoria reached her and instructed her to go knock on the neighbor's door for help. Thankfully, they managed to get the older woman to the nearby emergency hospital.

That incident, however pushed Victoria to share her

feelings about phone access with her employer. She decided to tell her boss it was very important to check on her phone, or call home during the day without the need to sneak into the toilet and feeling guilty about it afterwards.

She didn't have the courage to spill all this in front of her employer, of course, so she drafted a message in WattsApp instead. This way, she could express everything she wanted to say without being interrupted. She expressed how she felt tortured whenever her daughter called with questions about why she wouldn't talk regularly during the day, and how she didn't like being cut off from her family.

The next morning, Victoria sat in her employer's office expressing her concerns. Her heart was pounding so hard she could almost hear it beating. It was the first time she had openly expressed her emotions — and she was afraid she might be sent home. But she was wrong. Her employer apologized for making her suffer because of a house rule against daytime phone usage. They came to an agreement that she could use her phone a few minutes during the day. Victoria was happy — overjoyed — she had almost expected to be fired. But being able to communicate regularly with her family was what mattered most.

As time went on, Victoria was able to monitor her daughter's growth and development, getting updates about her studies. She was also able to help with difficult assignments and other projects, too, because they were able to exchange messages regularly. Victoria began to feel good about the job she was doing as a mother — all because of communication. She still works for the same employer, and has for many years, now. Together, they have managed to build a relationship that's built on respect, trust and, understanding.

Janelyn Dupingay is from Nueva Vizcaya, Philippines, and has been working in Singapore as a domestic helper since 2015. She came to love writing as it helps her release untold emotions, and it also became her way to connect with fellow migrants.Involved in different organizations that support the welfare of migrants, Jane was selected as one of the featured speakers for "A Labour of Love I: Spotlight in Tagalog" at the Singapore Writers Festival. In 2023, she published her poetry collection Language of My Heart.

PART 2
NON-FICTION

Lü Caiyi
Translated by Luka Lei Zhang

From Rubber Plantations to Construction Sites

1.Climbing up a Ladder to Cut Rubber (1977)

We harvested latex from old rubber trees, but the garden where the rubber trees stood was overgrown with weeds, and the bark on the lower parts of the tree trunks had already been stripped away. The latex was scarce; we had to use a ladder to climb up higher into the trees to pull away more bark and reach the latex underneath.

The ladder was made out of a kind of red bark, light wood from all kinds of local trees, because the boss simply refused to supply any lumber. It was about six feet high. Every morning, with a rubber knife in one hand and a ladder thrown over the left shoulder, we pushed aside dense weeds higher than a man's head that blocked the pathways into the garden. If it had rained the day before, the grass held water, and our clothes got so wet we couldn't tell the difference between sweat and rainwater. Inside the garden, we ran to the rubber trees, propped our ladders up against the trunks, and climbed up to do our work.

These ladders were prone to rotting, and were not very

durable. Once, when I climbed up and was trying to cut the gum, the ladder's crosspiece suddenly fell off — and I panicked. I grabbed at the tree trunk with my left hand, but then the rubber knife in my right hand jabbed me hard in the chest. Fortunately, it was not very deep. I immediately picked a plant shoot, put into the mouth, chewed it up with saliva, and put it on the wound to stop the bleeding. I was afraid that my mother would worry, so I hid it. She finally found out, and I was scolded.

Another worker on the plantation who also somehow fell off a ladder wasn't so lucky. When his grip slipped, the rubber knife fell and cut off one side of his nose. He was sent to the hospital for surgery.

2.Workers' Room (1977)

Rubber workers lived in a 300-foot-long dormitory. The rooms were as crowded as pigeon coops, packed with both rubber workers and their families. My mother, my siblings, and I lived in a room twelve-feet-long and ten-feet-wide. With a bed, a table, and a closet, there wasn't much room left for moving around.

In the beginning, we all slept in the same bed at night, which was inconvenient for us kids as we grew older. Eventually, my brother and I managed to put up a plank between the crossbeam. Every night, the two of us carefully climbed a ladder made out of nailed together tree limbs and slept on it. We curled up like cats in this makeshift bed as the night grew deeper, the fog thickened, and a deep chill came straight down through the roof. In the daytime, when the sun was blazing and the whole place was as hot as a steamer, we'd sweat profusely just in the short time it took to climb up; fortunately, we didn't take many naps.

I had also built a bookcase into the wall of this room where I hid a number of books by Johor Bahru, and others obtained by mail order from Singapore. Every day when I came back from cutting rubber, I hid in the room and read without leaving my house, which was quite enjoyable.

Later, some of the rubber workers bought their own houses and moved away. With the permission of the foreman, we moved to one of the empty rooms, finally ending years of awkwardness. I don't remember how long it took until we could afford to build our own house, and had a decent place we could call home!

3. A Junior Construction Worker (1978)

There was an oil palm plantation set up to help build new dormitories and the head builder in our village got the project. When the work on the wood factory was finished, I was transferred to help build dormitories.

The oil palm plantation and the village were exactly ten miles apart, and we all traveled back and forth on bikes every day. There is a hierarchy of workers in the construction industry. Those who have mastered a certain level of construction skill are considered senior workers who receive higher wages and are generally treated with "respect" by the foreman. Those who are new to the industry are called "junior workers." These odd-job workers are paid low wages, do the most heavy-duty work, and the senior workers can do whatever they want with them.

When I was in the wood factory, I only did the work of filling cement. I knew nothing else, so I could only act as a handyman. At the beginning of the construction, I was sweating like a pig, digging footings and carrying soil. When I was building the roof, I was carrying big logs and passing big tiles to the senior workers. My back was bent and my hands were bruised, but no one cares about you. Plastering is a time-critical job, and when it's happening, some senior workers become especially bad-tempered. Sometimes, they think the plaster is too soft, and other times they say it's too hard. If you don't do as you are told, they will throw your plaster on the floor with a bucket. It was very hard to deal with them. But if I took these problems to the foreman, I would be blamed.

A month or two slipped by in such working conditions, and still I had no chance of getting my hands on the technical work. When would I get a chance to master some construction skills? My anxiety and distress deepened day by day. How I longed to master those building techniques and get out of the predicament I was in. To be honest, I wasn't afraid of how hard the work was — what I couldn't stand was senior workers bossing us around!

One of the more easy-going senior workers told me that the foreman has to first believe I'm honest and reliable before he will even think about promoting me when he couldn't hire enough senior workers anymore. Then I'd have a chance to learn, he said.

"Why don't you ask your contractor friend to help you out," another senior worker said in a teasing tone.

These guys! One made me feel as if I was stuck in a long night not knowing when the day would break — while the other only made me only squeeze out a bitter smile.

Lü Caiyi was born in 1943 in Malaysia. Over the years, he has worked in rubber plantations and construction sites as a worker, and since 1985, he worked as a soybean milk hawker. He has had a strong interest in literature and writing from a young age. He has self-published two collections of his writings. His favorite writer is the renowned Chinese author Lu Xun.

Mengyu
Translated by Luka Lei Zhang

My Dagong Experiences

My name is Mengyu. I am from Pingliang, Gansu Province. I am 52 years old. For many years, I was a village woman who only knew how to cook, do housework, take care of the elderly and children in our family, and go out to do farm work in the field. I was used to following the life of the older generation of people who "faced the soil and turned their backs to the sky." I spent so many years repeating this monotonous and tedious routine, working from sunrise to sunset. Until 2005, when my husband's leg was severely injured in a car accident and the family's land was expropriated.

My three children attended school, and our parents were becoming older, the family had no income. My husband's temper became even worse because he had all of a sudden changed from a healthy person to a disabled person and would go into a rage at the drop of a hat. That year was also the lowest point in my life. In the second month after his accident, my sister died suddenly of a brain hemorrhage, and my mother also fell ill because of her grief. The successive blows made me, a lively and cheerful person, become less talkative and sullen. At that moment, I realized the meaning of the words, "Woe is not alone!"

In 2007, my two kids went to high school in the town one after another. In order to take care of them and earn some money for the family, I opened a steamed bun store in the small town. In the beginning, as I was not skillful, the business was not very good, and I couldn't earn much money, just barely enough to support the three of us. Slowly, the business got better and better, but I felt it was too busy to do it alone. The two kids came back to give me a hand after school. On weekends, when it was even busier, my youngest daughter, who was in elementary school in my home village, also came to help me. At that time, I always felt very busy. Sometimes, my relatives from the neighborhood showed up and helped, too. I had to do the work alone as well as delivering to the restaurants in the neighborhood. I was even busier when it came to weddings and funerals, and sometimes, I had to work all night long, which caused my children to suffer along with me. In 2011, my two older children went to college one after another. I felt that it was too tiring for me to work alone in the steamed bun store, so I transferred the business to someone else, and left with my kids to the city where they went to school. That's where I started my dagong life.

When I was at home, I often heard people say that a migrant worker's life is very hard. And yet, I thought it was not as hard as running a small business. But once I started working as a migrant worker, I realized that it is really hard! I got my first job in a beer factory, but because I lacked the necessary education and skills, I could only work in the recycling workshop. Every day, trucks would bring in used beer bottles, and we would have to check the bottles one by one to see if they were recyclable. If the bottles were broken, they had to be disposed. If they were filled with something, they had to be emptied out. You don't know how mean the drinkers are! Some bottles were filled with water, some with urine. If you didn't pay attention, you could pour a foot of it out, and it stank so bad! At that time, the factory was privately contracted, so we were only issued with overalls — no shoes. Our shoes and feet were often soaked at the end of the day. Our feet became soggy and white. Our shoes were soaked hard and wet. It was so uncomfortable! But it was still bearable for me. When I was young, I was afraid of nothing. I just wanted to earn more money. Nowadays, I get annoyed when I have dreams about the factory — the roar of the machine, the ear-piercing sound of glass bottles breaking, the loud scold of the shift manager. Oh, how he prevented us from talking to the truck drivers, always afraid that we worked too slow, constantly monitoring us.

I remember once when I was loading the bottles into boxes, one of the boxes fell from the top and hit my foot, the box contained sixteen beer bottles, which directly smashed onto my big toe. I couldn't get up from the floor, I couldn't bear the pain, but I didn't dare cry. I was afraid that the shift manager would see me, and ask me to go home. It was already almost winter. There were fewer beer bottles to collect and many workers at the factory, so they wanted to lay off some people and recruit again in the coming year when the weather got warmer and there were more beer drinkers and more recycled bottles. So that day, I had to wrap my wound with toilet paper, put on socks to endure the pain, and continue to work. My big toe has still not been healed and has left a sequela.

Later that same year, when I returned home for Chinese New Year, my husband saw the scars on my body and would no longer let me go to work in the factory. So, after the break, I went to Yinchuan to work, as I heard people in my village say that the wages in Yinchuan were high and that I could earn more than 200 yuan a day as a caregiver in the hospital. In order to pay for my two children's schooling, I went to the hospital to work as a caregiver. When I got there, I told myself that no matter how hard and tiring it was, I would persevere to the end and earn more money. But I felt ashamed that I couldn't persevere after a month of working in the hospital. I could tolerate the hard work and the late nights, but after taking care of patients who could not move, wiping up their urine and shit, my stomach would turn over and I would vomit. I could not eat a single mouthful of food. I was already particularly thin and weak. It was not that I disliked the patients, but I just couldn't get used to it. I felt like fainting when I stepped out of the hospital and saw the sun. Looking at my pale face in and my body in the mirror, I knew that I couldn't do it any longer. It wasn't cost-effective for me to continue to destroy my body like this, without health, how could I earn a living to support my family? So, I decided to change my job again. I remember that on the day I left, the old man whom I had taken care of for almost a month pulled my hand to keep me from leaving. The memory is still vivid in my mind. I guess that I am incapable of enduring adversities and hard work. Others can work tirelessly, but I cannot — which is exactly what my father said when he was alive and described me as a "servant girl with princess syndrome."

Later, I learned from people in my village that domestic service is a good industry. I then went to look for a domestic helper agency. Because I lacked experience, I tried a few duties as a domestic worker, but none worked out. Either because the standards were too strict or the wages were too low to attain my ideal. It took a lot of time and effort, but it also made me feel like a headless fly. I didn't make any money, and in return, I felt so lost in life.

Am I really so useless? Am I always unlucky? I have doubts about life, I do not know what I should do? I asked myself over and over again in my mind.

At this time, the "Mother's Lecture" came to our village to hold an event. The president of the Women's Federation, as well as the village officials mobilized me to go to the lecture as a way of taking a break. I went with the mentality of just trying something to cope with my situation. But as I sat in the venue, I became deeply attracted to the insightful lectures and psychological guidance being offered. My worries eased. It gave me confidence and courage, especially the simple words of the president, "Only self-confidence can save you." They are still fresh in my mind. I remember at the end of the day the president of the County Women's Federation told us about the organization's "working brand" and its poverty alleviation programs. Each one sounded nice and intimate. We all felt very warm. When they mentioned the domestic helper transfer training program, I was fascinated, especially since after completing the training, one can be employed in Beijing. I quickly signed up because visiting Beijing, the capital city, had always been a childhood dream of mine. How wonderful it would be to see Tiananmen Square, the Forbidden City, and the Great Wall in my spare time!

Under the coordination of the County Women's Federation, a group of more than 40 sisters and I set out on the road to Beijing for employment, and after a week of intense training at the Fuping Training School, I quickly found a job. I have now worked for more than three years, during which time I have raised a small baby from infancy. The child is healthy, energetic, and adorable. My employer's family and I understand each other, respect each other, and trust each other. My monthly income has increased from 4,000 yuan to 6,000 yuan — and I have achieved the transformation from a rural woman to a professional woman!

In Beijing, female domestic workers have been recognized as professional women and are respected by society, especially our Gansu "Longyuan women." We are recognized and appreciated by the industry for our simplicity, kindness and dedication. I would like to thank my sisters in the industry; we have won such recognition through our hard work. I would also want to thank the leaders of the county Women's Federation for their strong support and help, without which I would not have been able to develop the abilities of a rural woman into valuable contributions to society.

After I started working in Beijing, I had a day off every week. During that time, I joined the Beijing Home of Hongyan social work organization on the recommendation of my friends. I have met numerous other domestic workers there. Under the direction of the staff, we formed a cultural group to make the most of our free time by learning and entertaining together, allowing the sisters to relax and better serve their employers. So far, my sisters and I have not only used our leisure time to enhance ourselves, but we have also brought joy and confidence to more people and improved our sisters' comprehension and affirmation of the domestic service industry.

The Beijing Hongyan Social Work Service Centre is a professional social work organization that promotes women's empowerment and community development. It was founded in September 2014, and officially recognized as a non-governmental organization in May 2016. It is based in the Dawangjing area of Chaoyang, Beijing, and its current projects focus on community services, research, and advocacy for women, mostly domestic workers, to promote social integration and equal growth in urban society. In addition to community services, Home of Hongyan focuses on the cultivation of talents and the longterm development of community organizations through professional video production, theatre practice, feminist writing, and other collaborative social work methods. It collaborates with them by developing creative courses and providing systematic training. We, female domestic workers from all across the country, rely on Home of Hongyan to ease our worries and psychological burdens and allow us to perform our tasks pleasantly.

While relaxing, I picked up my pen after a long time, and recorded my journey with words, as well as every bit of my study and work in Beijing. In Beijing Picun Workers' Home, I got to know many famous teachers and fellow writers who shared the same hobby of writing literary works and joined a literary group with them to learn to write together, to discuss the confusions I encountered in my life, and to share the changes and joys that writing brought to all of us. With the support and encouragement of teachers and friends, my poems have been published many times on New Workers' Literature and Jianjiao Tribe. Under the guidance of my example, twenty-two female domestic workers who passed the training program organized by the County Women's Federation in 2018 have all found satisfactory jobs in Beijing.

In January 2017, my domestic worker sisters and I took part in the first "Hundred Hands Supporting the Family" (Baishou chengjia) Domestic Women Workers' Art Festival, which was organized by the staff of Hongyan Social Work Service Centre. We also took part in the online performance of the Chinese New Year Festival Gala for Working People on Phoenix TV, and our original improvised dance performance of Dancing in Labour received a lot of praise. In January 2018, I spoke about my job and growth experiences at the Provincial Women's Federation's New Year's Gala, where I also performed on stage and received the prestigious title of "Outstanding Longyuan Woman" from the Federation. In November 2018, on the recommendation and guidance of director Dong Dalu, I appeared on the stage of "Super Speaker 2018" to advocate for my female domestic workers. I took photos with the famous actress Liu Xiaoqing, who was present as a supervisory teacher, and was honored to be given a book autographed by Ms. Liu.

In July 2019, our domestic sisters established the "Mei Mei Da" literary group under the guidance of the Hongyan Social Work Service Centre. We invited teachers to assist us in writing lyrics and songs, and participated in the Mulan Women Workers'Art Festival, where we created our own song (Hongyan Mama). Our song won first place, while our dance came in third. These small rewards boost our self-confidence and excitement for the domestic service industry. In October 2019, we were also invited to participate in the sixth garden art festival activities; this is our Hongyan Mei Mei Da arts group's third interesting activity, and as non-professional domestic workers, we felt very honored. We were also invited to a New Year's Day party hosted by a Beijing domestic service company and the Home of the Working Girls, where we sang and danced together to celebrate our holiday.

The Hongyan Social Workers' Service Centre organized another unique activity for us at the end of October this year: The Second Art Festival for Women Domestic Workers. This activity is the fruit of three years of meticulous planning by Mei Ruo, the main organizer of Hongyan House, and her team, who overcame numerous unknown challenges to organize it. There were not only speeches by our female domestic workers themselves, but also original songs and dances with the help of the teachers of the New Workers' Troupe and Jiuye Band.

We also released the album Encounter of Lives, which was recorded by our domestic worker sisters. The album featured the stories of 3500 female domestic workers on stage. Over 170,000 people watched the concert online and it was supported by various media outlets. We domestic workers were so moved and delighted.

Working as a domestic worker allows me to pursue my aspirations. It also demonstrates my value and contributions to society. My two sons have now found satisfying jobs, while my daughter is learning hairdressing skills and hopes to open her own salon in the future. My family has also gotten out of the trap, my husband has found a suitable job with the support of friends and family. Things are gradually changing. The journey of dagong is rough and tiring, but also full of joy and excitement; it makes me feel that everything is leading somewhere, and there is a never-ending drive to push me on....

Mengyu is from Gansu province, China. She was born in 1966 and works as a domestic worker. As part of the Picun Literary Collective in Beijing, her poems and illustrations have been featured in various magazines and platforms. Mengyu is currently working on her first illustration book focused on domestic workers in China.

Shengzi

Translated by Luka Lei Zhang

Notes from the Factory

Entry 1 2011.09.02 16:00-24:00

The two production lines, which had been separated due to a variety of unfavorable conditions, were brought back together utilizing a considerable number of human and material resources. A few workers had to be let go. Two workers have been replaced by one, and the task has been doubled without wage increases. The level of automation is low, and the computers used for operation act just as switches and knobs; there are no additional workers to support the process, and a great amount of labor must be completed by a single person. Stress levels and emotions among workers have become sensitive and irritable as a result of the tension. There were already fewer people, but the number has now decreased even further. Centralized operations and administration, which reduce privacy while increasing control, have now become the primary style of operation in the factory. Every day, the shift changeover is like a drama, seeing coworkers argue in the main control room, close by but not knowing what they were talking over, only seeing their changing expressions, their hands gesticulating, and their feet exerting force, but not knowing where to point it. It took approximately ten minutes. They were not personally entangled in any manner, they just argued. They argued as a form of release. They had no scruples, they said anything they wanted, and displayed their anger. The dispute is only about work. After the fight, if there is no director or boss there, they will "move their necks and hug their waists" like sisters, chatting about family affairs and cursing others.

For instance:
The unlucky weasel. (A vice chairman with the surname Huang, he is slender and small, so everyone calls him that behind his back).
How come he is not blind in that eye? (A work-related injury left a coworker blind in one eye).
A good dog never looks back. (A coworker once resigned and was rehired).

Entry 2   2011.09.03 16:00-24:00

As usual, there is a lot of noise during shift changes, but once you begin to work, there is a lot of silence. At the moment, however, we may relax a little, and there is a lot of joking and cursing. The most common complaint is that the job was too tiring. "What, Lao Yang, can't you drive slower? You're the only one who is this capable! You drive so quickly every day." The liquid level was too high, and it bubbled up in the blink of an eye, while saying so, they covered their lips and laughed, claiming that it bubbled up twice, and then they laughed wildly again. Alternatively, they claim that the "officials" speak too rudely. This is an old narrative, but it still plays out daily, and will continue. The main control room has a variety of tastes and is vibrant. Wang Fang is carrying a 30kg blue plastic bucket of additives in one hand, her face filled with rage and hatred, yet this does not appear to be her personality. It is in the factory workshop where individuals become deformed. Once you're here, you're like a balloon that can be twisted into unusual shapes. The workshop contains such soil.
I arrived at the factory early today, before the shift, and there was still time for chatting. Chatting can lead to some disputes. People and things in the factory are complicated, and there are many disagreements among coworkers, but most of the time we just talk about it, in our own words, and the unclear and undirected waves will vanish

without our knowing.

Every day, Ah Wen would yell at the steel tank, whether the liquid level was high or low. The liquid level circulated and clattered in a circular motion, workers became terror-stricken. When the raw materials transformed into industrial liquids, circulating and flowing in steel tanks, they were hit by the machines and had the momentum of the industry. How many people's youth have been lost in this never-ending pounding? Steel pipes and empty factories have a tremendous noisy force.

Wang Fang returned from her inspection; she had to pass through the steel spiral staircase and the massive tanks; above her head was the dense pipeline; the sound gushing from the pipeline was powerful, like a snake that regained its senses in the spring and swam on the wheat lawns. Those hot and cold liquids thus gained a form, but they were ignored in the wear and tear of the day, and they were no longer a bit of freshness. She has been doing the same job for almost ten years, and her bored eyes are still withdrawn, the routine is the same every day, and her worries are the same. She clicks to start, run, forward, or reverse, but there is no door, window, or shelter in the workshop, which remains to be constructed. Noise and dust come and fall at our feet...we are used to it.

Entry 3 2011.09.04 08:00-16:00

Midday is the most sleepy time of day, and the sound of steel drains the spirit. The main control room remains open, with dispersed aluminum bars, frames, and glasses that haven't been installed. The sound of human voices cannot be heard from the opposite side of the room. Every day, they yell with their necks until their voices are muffled like scraping iron sheets. Data transmission appears to be a constant issue, either incorrectly or not audible. The walkie-talkie tumbles around, "The things in the factory are so durable," well, you cannot destroy it easily. Smashing the walkie-talkie is a really happy thing; annoyed by the fallout, on the ground, a long slide, rubbing the floor, rolling. You can just smash it when you are in a bad mood. It just falls on the ground and rolls on.

Then, you can pick it up with a smile when you are in a better mood. Computers and telephones cannot be smashed, while walkie-talkies are the most helpful and relieving since they constantly generate noise.

The operation is not running smoothly today. Occasionally, the pump wouldn't turn on, at other times the screw plate jammed, and a few times it was going to bubble up, which it did once. They screamed, then covered their mouths and dashed for the broom, screaming, "It's bad luck if the weasel sees it." There's a devilish delight in not being caught. The water tank's valve has suddenly failed, and the water spills out of the opening and rushes along, cheerfully taking over the entire platform. Uncontaminated water is beautifully clear. Wang Wei rushes up quickly after passing beneath the platform and becoming drenched. The jumping and screaming water water ignores Wang Wei's flurry. The pump stops and the water level drops. There is no trace on the platform.

Fortunately, no one is around, so everyone is happy to indulge.

Entry 4   2011.09.05 08:00-16:00

The work site has become a construction site again, and it so happens, the Municipal Federation of Trade Unions has come for a visit (either for inspection or to pay tribute). But why? This workers' organization has entirely degraded into a government department. It has no interaction with the workers and does not communicate with them. Representing the interests of the government and the bosses instead. If they did nothing, they might not turn into maggots, but aren't they merely advising the bosses? The core function of trade unions has been emasculated, and I'm afraid they can only be called "eunuch" organizations. What is the relationship between trade unions and workers? A group of well-dressed, fat-brained people with the news media, like Wen xx, visited the grassroots. At least the old Wen will have to speak to the masses decently, whereas the eunuchs only have eyes for the officials and bosses. Perhaps they will also consider themselves to be government officials.

The situation was chaotic since it was still under construction, and no one had time to clean it up in the middle of a hectic workday. The bosses and their trade union officials were all talking to each other, while the camera focused on the bosses' glowing faces. This is such a classic scene, and it appears that the trade union's visit to the grassroots in order to soothe frontline workers will be a major piece of news this evening. The Mid-Autumn Festival is approaching, so they need to get out and do something. I'm not sure which factory manager will pay the bill, but that's not something we'll be concerned about.

The best has yet to come. After they left, the workshop manager was furious, charging that we had not adequately cleaned up the scene. He had lost face, which was terrible.

"I've been so busy all the time, how can I clean it?" Xiao Yang said. And they said, "You can stop working for a while, but you must clean it up." Do the workers dare stop the production line to clean up the site? Can the machines be stopped? That is something we would want to do. But that's only a word for these stupid people. Workers are so small that they must listen to everything. Both good and terrible. Direct and indirect. And they have to understand what it means. The shift supervisor then approached and said, "After work, you guys have to clean up all the hygiene and miscellaneous items on the site, as well as the staircases and other vacant rooms that don't belong to our hygiene area. You will be fined 50 yuan for not doing so." He'll come and check them out after cleaning.

Entry 5   2011.09.08 00:00-08:00

The machine in operation is constantly failing in one way or another. With a shredding capacity of around 300 tons every shift, energy consumption and wear are huge — with stones, iron, mud, and plant debris. Unidentified iron items rushing through the air ducts have long been the norm. Forward or reverse, the blades fly through the machine, the destructive blades are destroyed, and the shredder eliminates the grumpy hours. At 4 a.m., the shredder goes down with a gasp. Ah Fong makes some noises, while the tired watchman, the wobbling electrician, the feverish electrical equipment, the mechanical brake system, and the forklift driver all take advantage of the opportunity to go into a sound sleep.

The inverter motor moves forward, the inverter motor moves backward. Launch the frequency converter. Iron pieces are striking, struggling, and ultimately running up. The assembly line resumes operation. Liu Zhiyuan's shiny bald head is drenched in sweat.

The mouse began to click, and the machine, which had previously lifted the red alarm, begins to flicker frequently again.

Entry 6 2011.09.09 00:00-08:00

There is nothing more terrifying here than the word "clean." This is the main control room, a dusty industrial production site. How can the windows remain clear and clean? So come on, comrade workers, just do a good job. Wipe, wipe, wipe. The industrial area does not believe in tears, as long as you work hard, and sacrifice the rest to work, working in "five plus two, white plus black" mode. (Editor's Note: Workers do not rest on weekends, and work both day and night. This phrase is used as a part of corporate culture and in government reports to promote working culture).

Liu Zhiyuan says, "I get dizzy when I see the floor." Yang Wenju says, "Mum! It is as clean as a funeral parlor. The forklift driver says, "Son, I don't dare to enter." The floors and ceiling are white, and there is soundproof glass. Outside, there are marble stairs with stainless steel railings. The 100-square-meter main control room is like a gym. Do it right, guys...this is where your nightmares begin! We prefer that it be small, dirty, rough, architecturally neutral, unfurnished, and easy to clean.

"Clean and clear" is a ballache phrase!

Entry 7 2011.09.10 16:00-24:00

The Mid-Autumn Festival will be celebrated in two days. I

have spent it on the assembly line every year for more than 20 years, with almost no exceptions, except for production halts or holidays.

Workers do not have holidays. The factories have become increasingly indifferent to those who work on holidays. The moon in mid-autumn is destined to rust and hang on the steel railings.

The metal moon is cool when the wind blows. Is the unappreciated moon another moon?

The moon is running in the sky; perhaps she has a performance indicator as well, given her punctuality.

Shengzi was born in 1968 in Jiangsu province, China. Shengzi is a pseudonym, and all his works are published under this name. The author prefers to be known and introduced with this name. He started working in a state-owned factory producing ethyl alcohol in 1988 and worked in different factories for twenty years. Shengzi has been dedicating himself to working-class literature since 2000 by writing poems and organizing online forums for worker literature. Most of his poems are directly related to his working experiences, offering a critical voice of an exploited working-class collective.

Julie Ann
A Cherished Experience

Family is...

The people in your life who want you in theirs; the ones who accept you for who you are, love you no matter what, and would do anything to see you smile.

I grew up in a beautiful island in the Philippines where fishing is the main source of living. My father is a fisherman and was only renting a boat. My mother is a plain housewife, though sometimes, she does some sideline jobs to lessen our financial burden. I have five siblings. One of my sisters went back home to heaven when she was just six-years-old.

Being the eldest in the family, I witnessed my parents' difficulties caused by poverty. I felt a sting of pain whenever I saw my father's sun-burned skin or a cut of nylon on his hand from fishing. My mother has aged more than her actual age because she struggled to make the money fit into our everyday needs. Because I was still studying on that time, I promised myself that when I grew older and became stronger I would help them with their financial problems. In that way, I could reciprocate them for the sacrifices they made for us.

Actually, it wasn't my dream to work abroad. I dreamed of becoming a teacher because aside from being keen on children, I believe that having a stable job and good pay is a way to survive life. Unfortunately, I didn't finish my studies due to financial problems. I have no choice now but to try my luck and find greener pastures in a foreign land. Especially since I've become a mother. Fear whispers in my ears to stop. But my determination pushes me through. I first laid eyes on the beauty of Singapore on June 7, 2013. I was mesmerized by the tall buildings, the trees inside the airport, everything new and exciting. I experienced a mixture of anxiety and happiness. Especially when I saw the people walking in front of me. I was awed by their beauty and color that is so different from my own brown skin tone. When I looked at my reflection in the glass door, I was scared. But I remained rooted to my purpose, although I was away from my son.

In the beginning of my contract, I shed lots of tears. But those tears become a silent prayer for me to be able to cope. It became my strength to endure the pain of being away from my loved ones, and to slowly adapt to my environment. I cannot back out. I don't have the money to compensate the loan I took out from my agency; only six months of receiving an allowance to sustain my basic necessities. I focus on my work and try to be responsible in my duties to win their trust. Even the ten cents I found inside a pocket while doing laundry will be returned to them. I wake up before the sun rises to start my day. I chant a prayer of "everything will be fine" to finish the day until I doze off at my comfort place — a bed that caresses my swollen heart and my stiff muscles and gets me ready again for the next day. Soon, perhaps, life abroad will become bearable.

After a year, my own family fell apart. We were not on the same page. I was not his priority. So, I decided to go back to my family whose love and care I was longing for. They accepted me without hesitation and asked me what happened. Some people in his place looked at me with disgust — like I had an incurable disease. And yet, it didn't shake me because I know my own story. I know my reasons. Their actions became my source of inspiration and strength to battle on in life. I believe that the truth will reveal and unfold in its own perfect time.

I pursued my long overdue promise to my parents. I started to save my salary, and was the happiest I've ever been when I saw my father's smile reach his eyes after I bought his longtime dream — a motor boat (banca de motor)! My family's bahay kubo is reconstructed into something that is comfortable to live in even during raining or typhoon seasons.

Now, I worry less. Last month, I bought a small piece of land which we will develop into a small business for my retirement one day.

The journey is not easy, especially from where I am starting. I brought bread with kaya spread and a bottle of water and sat in a corner waiting for my curfew to go back and work again. It's a celebration for me whenever I have seven dollars to treat myself to a meal in Jollibee. I am doing this not to pity myself, but to save until my goals were achieved.

Now, I am slowly breathing with ease because I can see some changes in my family's way of living, but the most important thing for us is to remain humble. All thanks to God for giving me the courage to pursue my dreams for my family. Without his gift of wisdom and his guidance, I don't know where I would be today.

I still want to do something for my parents...to bring them here to Singapore one day and experience the beauty which made me fall in love...to see the bridge to achieving my dreams. I want them to see the beautiful Island of Sentosa, which I know they will love. Its white sandy shore, sparkling waters, and roaming around inside the studios. I want to let them taste the local food in hawker center — especially chicken rice, which is my favorite. I can't wait for them to feel the ambience and relaxation of this small red dot, which offers so many wonders and fascinating experiences.

I also want to secure my son's future which always is my top priority. As a mother, it's my duty to support his endeavors in life anyway I can. Distance is not a hindrance to make him feel that I am always with him in every season of his journey. And to remind myself that he is the reason for all of these sacrifices. Seeing him successful in the future will be worth the sweat and blood of being a mother away from her precious son.

Success is still far away. However, when I see my parents smile, and how proud they are, it gives me assurance that I am on the right path.

Julie Ann is a mother, a team leader and one of the volunteers of Migrant Writers of Singapore and she loves hosting. Her poem titled "Love Yourself" is included in the Sixth Edition of The Tiger Moth Eco Review and "Car" was published in an anthology book Warm Tea on Rainy Day. She also performed on several stages and the most recent was in the Asian Civilization auditorium during Singapore's Writers Festival.

Md Sharif Uddin

Stranger Life in Singapore

Since the independence of Singapore, migrant workers have been brought from different countries for the sake of the development of this country. Migrant workers have also come to this country and loved this country. In the 21st century, they are still trying their best for the development of this country. For example, the contribution of migrant workers behind the building of today's modern Singapore is very high — buildings that stand tall within this country today. The sacrifices of migrant workers and the sweat of work-weary bodies are behind the construction of the city that has made Singapore a role model of environmental cleanliness.

Migrant workers are very important to this country. About one-third of the total population are expatriates. Each worker leaves their family members behind out of financial necessity. The agents come to Singapore for a fee after being trained in various subjects. They leave their families and work for months and years, hiding their burdens. Many turn from young to old to fulfill their family's dreams. Many dreams come true. Many die at work, leaving their families in a precarious existence.

However, the life of migrant workers in this country is not easy. They live in this country through their utmost sacrifice. They are largely deprived of their natural rights, which becomes very difficult to endure. Many migrant workers live subhuman lives in dormitories across this country. I am a worker like them.

After working tirelessly all day, I get restless to return to the room. Then an unwanted pain brings tears to the corners of my eyes. It feels good to stretch your body in your bed and relax. But then that room becomes hell. It is hot, and the stench of sweat from the bodies of thirty-six people makes the pulse turn upside down. There is a state of choking. The distance from the living room to the wash room is about 200 meters. Drink less water to reduce urination. In the past 15 years of expatriation, I have never encountered such a strange situation. This confined environment of the dormitory is driving me almost crazy.

I can't sleep comfortably even for a moment at night. In summer, the bed gets wet with sweat from the whole body. I clean it with a towel and try to sleep again. More mental torture begins. Many people do not sleep due to snoring. Sometimes I wake up suddenly due to a rat. Someone is watching a movie on a loud mobile phone. Someone is talking loudly on another mobile phone. Many workers cannot stay in the room and go to sleep on the balcony. Just like there are many dogs lying around on the road!

Early in the morning, they leave the back of the lorry for work with sleepless eyes. Hard work all day again. Going back to that dormitory hell again. One night is like a hundred years! This is how time passes. Here the underprivileged laborers cover their woes with sighs. They know there is no use telling the owners. The difference between and owner's life and laborer's life is clearly understood in this country. Migrant workers in this country live like wounded jackals.

Actually, in this country the workers are hostage to the owners. There is no value in asking workers. The owners manage the workers as they wish. The owners want only work, and more work. They consider workers as machines. But workers are also human beings made of flesh and blood. They also need adequate rest. Adequate food is required. Owners do not understand the need for adequate sleep.

On holidays, I walk outside all day. At night, on my way back to the dormitory, I look at the beautiful tall buildings of this country and sigh. The citizens of this country are sleeping peacefully and comfortably in the buildings built by us. What a beautiful and tidy life they have. But we live under the same sky. We spend the night in restlessness with tired bodies. How much we yearn for a little restful sleep. How much suffering we are passing the time; like the life of a servant. In this modern city we are locked in the chains of subjugation. I don't know when we will become people and not just workers! When will the migrant workers of this country lead a good life?

Md Sharif Uddin was born on 5 September 1978 in Dilalpur village, Nandail, Mymensingh, Bangladesh to MD Dulal Bhuiyan and Renu Ara Begum. He has a Diploma in Ceramic Technology. He arrived in Singapore in 2008 where he works in the construction and tunneling sectors as a supervisor. Sharif writes short stories and poetry and his works have been published in journals and anthologies in Singapore and Bangladesh. His first book, Stranger to Myself, won the Singapore Book Award in the non-fiction category, in 2018.